NATE COFFIN'S REVENGE

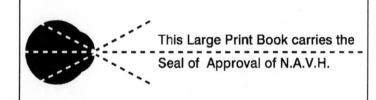

This Large Print Book carries the
Seal of Approval of N.A.V.H.

LUCIUS DODGE
AND THE BORDER BANDITS

NATE COFFIN'S REVENGE

J. LEE BUTTS

WHEELER PUBLISHING
A part of Gale, Cengage Learning

GALE
CENGAGE Learning

Detroit • New York • San Francisco • New Haven, Conn • Waterville, Maine • London

GALE
CENGAGE Learning™

LIBRARY OF CONGRESS CATALOGING-IN-PUBLICATION DATA

Butts, J. Lee (Jimmy Lee)
    Nate Coffin's revenge : Lucius Dodge and the border bandits
/ by J. Lee Butts.
        p. cm. — (Wheeler Publishing large print western)
    ISBN-13: 978-1-59722-740-7 (pbk. : alk. paper)
    ISBN-10: 1-59722-740-4 (pbk. : alk. paper)
    1. Texas — Fiction. 2. Large type books. I. Title.
PS3602.U893N37 2008
813'.6—dc22   2008002904

Published in 2008 by arrangement with The Berkley Publishing Group, a member of Penguin Group (USA) Inc.

Printed in the United States of America
1 2 3 4 5 6 7 12 11 10 09 08

ACKNOWLEDGMENTS

Special thanks to my friend and agent, Kimberly Lionetti, for her limitless patience and understanding of a rapidly aging old grump. My gratitude to Berkley Editor, Samantha Mandor, for her amazing ability to respond to my every request. And finally a tip of the Stetson to my good buddy, Red Shuttleworth, a great poet of the West, who always manages to pick my sagging spirits up with a simple phone call.

"Bad men live that they may eat and drink, whereas good men eat and drink that they may live."
— Plutarch, *How a Young Man Ought to Hear Poems*

"I have found power in the mysteries of thought,
exaltation in the chanting of the Muses;
I have been versed in the reasonings of men;
but Fate is stronger than anything I have known."
— Euripides, *Alcetis,* 1.962

PROLOGUE

Lucius Dodge's Sulphur River ranch near Domino, Texas, November 1948

Got right chilly last night. Bit unusual for Texas this time of year. Put me in mind of a frost-covered outhouse seat in Montana. Lord have mercy, but I do hate the cold.

Horse killer of a Blue Norther swept in so fast three days ago, some animals died in mid-stride, front half frothy and the back half frozen. Icy winds hit my ancient, decrepit body like a sledgehammer. Forced me to give up agreeable evenings on the screened-in back porch where I like to sit and contemplate the tumultuous events of my past.

Leaves shriveled up and fell off the trees more than a month ago. Starkly naked limbs click and clack against each other in the wind like bones dancing in a graveyard. Grass withered, turned into an ugly brown carpet that crunches when I hobble out to

11

the barn to check on my animals. Sun done went and hid its face behind thick, dark clouds — most days anyway. Everything in nature just kind of drew up into itself — like me.

Been forced to hibernate here in the house next to my stoked-up tin stove. Damned thing actually glows when encouraged in just the right fashion. Going through firewood like popped corn. As is the case with most old men who live alone, got nothing to do during such times 'cept ruminate and remember.

Don't know about nobody else, but I've always liked hot weather. Full-bore summertime's exactly my cup of tea. Hotter than hell under a frying pan's the way my old friend Hayden Tilden used to describe my preference for sizzling days and blazing sunshine.

Think about ole Tilden often lately. He once told me as how — sometimes at night — a particularly vivid nightmare could snatch him out of a sound sleep like a magician he once saw what jerked a white rabbit from the bottom of a stovepipe hat. Often as not, said he'd snap awake and see Death slouched at the foot of his hospital bed tapping fleshless, bony fingers against a sharpened, ebony-handled scythe. Said the gruesome vision's silver blade glistened in the moonlight with the bloody remnants of countless unsuspecting souls snatched to the other side by the grinning bastard. Sends shivers through my ancient leather-tough heart just thinking about that ghostly phantom and his single-minded mission to relieve me of my earthly spirit.

Have come to believe that perhaps such fantastic images are just typical of creeping old age and the inevitable rendezvous we all have with God's grim servant. Must confess I've not seen the skeletal apparition inside my bedroom — leastways not yet. But you know, must admit that a time or two of late, I have spotted that sneaky thief of spirits as he darted amongst the trees between my house and the river, or hid in my stand of huckleberry bushes and spied on me.

Seems to me as how ole Bony Fingers was always around somewhere back when me and Boz Tatum chased badmen all over Hell and Texas during my stint as a Ranger. Know for damned sure I saw him the day we caught up with Dolphus Twiggens out on the Wichita, not far from the Indian Nations, back in '80, or maybe '82. Being as how I've never told anyone this particular tale before, I'd appreciate it if you wouldn't repeat what you're about to hear.

Day it happened, Boz sat a fine sorrel horse named Sunset and pointed to grayish-white wafts of smoke that drifted from a rough cabin's chimney. Sagging live oaks, sad in their silence, hid most of a board-and-batten shack sheltered in a cup of grassy earth. Front porch looked rotted, and a pair of run-out broomtails drooped from fatigue in the ramshackle corral, a few paces from one end of the broken-down hovel.

My friend glanced at me, smiled, and said, "Bet you a frosty beer at the White Elephant Saloon we've done went and found the crazy bastard's hidey-hole."

Pulled my belly gun, flipped the loading gate open, and rolled the cylinder past each chamber. Everything looked in order. Said, "Ain't bettin' with you this time, Boz. When last we went out, I ended up owin' you for more beer than I could drink up in a month of Sundays. Hell, you got a week's worth of free liquor off me with that rainbow of a rifle shot when you killed Albert Scruggs."

He stifled a low chuckle and checked over his own weapons. "Well, damn, Lucius, you just ain't no fun a-tall. Noticed as how you been grumpier'n a sixty-year-old bachelor the closer we've got to cornerin' Dolphus."

"Could be," I said. "Been thinkin' on how we've never run too many others to ground as deadly as this man-killin' son of a bitch."

My blue roan, Grizz, shifted and stamped a white-socked foot. Shook his head, then grunted. Always believed that animal had the power of second sight. Most folks gave that notion little credit, but Grizz somehow seemed to know when trouble loomed ahead. Had got to a point where I trusted his equine judgment, but must admit it bothered me some the way he acted. Just never knew what to expect when he got jumpy as a bit-up bull in fly time.

Boz holstered the last of three pistols he carried on his belt, slid his shotgun out of its bindings, breeched the big popper, and examined both heavy loads. "True enough," he said. "Don't recall ever havin' to take a man down what kilt four people with a double-bit ax." He snapped the weapon shut with a loud metallic pop and laid it across his saddle for death-dealing handiness.

"Talked with Hardy Forrest 'fore we rode out of Fort Worth, Boz. He's the Ranger what found them poor boys. Said it was the worst mess he'd ever seen in all his days of investigatin' murders." Followed my partner's lead and checked my sawed-off blaster as well.

"Yeah. I spoke with Hardy too. Man told

me as how it looked like someone slaughtered half a dozen hogs in that shack. Even found bloody flesh, teeth, hair, and an eyeball or three stuck on the ceiling. Glad I didn't have to see any of it."

My friend's rendition of Ranger Forrest's assessment of Dolphus Twiggens's murderous efforts drew a cold, wordless shroud over our conversation. Noticed hardened lines at the corners of Boz's eyes. Detected an involuntary twitch near the edge of a cracked lip.

He lifted his animal's reins, gently brought Mexican spurs against its flanks, and said, "Well, let's ease on down and corral the evil son of a bitch. Gonna give me more'n a little pleasure watchin' him hang for what he went and done."

"Think he'll fight, Boz?"

He shook his head and urged Sunset forward. "Doubt it, but ain't no way to know for certain sure. Near as I've been able to tell, the man never hurt a fly up till the day he chopped up all them poor folks. Personally, never even knew of him to carry a gun. But you cain't ever tell what any man's gonna do when confronted with the possibility of his own mortality at the end of a rope. Guess we'll damned sure see how dangerous ole Twiggens is in a few minutes."

16

We moseyed down the gentle, grass-covered slope, and drew our animals up near one end of the cabin's dilapidated porch. Stopped behind a stack of firewood decorated with a heavy growth of thick moss. Got settled and Boz yelled out, "Dolphus Twiggens. This is Ranger Boz Tatum. You know why I'm here. Bring your murderous self outside — right now."

Something huge and heavy moved behind the shack's thin walls. Door cracked open on dried-out leather hinges that complained under the weight of unpainted wood. Brought my shotgun up and propped the butt against an aching leg. Thickly bearded man, the size of a Concord coach, stepped onto the creaking plank porch and turned, kind of sideways, toward us — half in and half out of the entryway. Whole building appeared to tip up and sag his direction.

Under my breath, and out of the corner of my mouth, I whispered, "Sweet jumpin' Jesus, Boz. That's the biggest human being I've ever seen. No one bothered to mention ole Dolphus might have some grizzly bear in his family tree."

"He's a big 'un all right. Must be a six-and-a-half-footer. Bet he weighs upward of three hundred pounds. But far as I've ever heard, big ole boy's sweet-natured as a well-fed house cat — long as he ain't had nothin' to drink."

Creature on the porch eyeballed us for a spell before he finally spoke. Dark, bushy brows knotted over a flat nose when he growled, "Ain't goin' back with you 'uns, Ranger Tatum. Them folks in town will hang me fer what I went and done. Sure as death, taxes, and Texas."

My partner shook his head. Sounded almost sympathetic when he said, "You gotta come with us, Dolphus. No way around it. We'll take you to Fort Worth. See you get a fair trial. Can't promise what'll happen after that."

Twiggens's fur-covered chin dropped to his slab-sized chest. He swayed back and forth like some kind of massive puppy dog, puzzled over a newly discovered scorpion.

Surprised the hell out of me when Boz said, "Will you let us come a bit closer? Never cared to spend my time yellin' at anyone."

Twiggens pawed the tangled mess of hair on his head, then scratched at the front of a ragged shirt. "Don't make me no difference where 'bouts you sit, Tatum. Come on over, if'n that's what you boys want."

Boz clucked at Sunset, urged the hay burner around the pile of stove wood and up to the edge of the porch. I followed, but immediately felt uneasy about the less than ten feet that separated us from the object of our nearly two-week search. Didn't appear to matter how we approached. The bulky giant kept his right side turned away from us, and kind of danced, from foot to foot, in a childlike fidget.

"Ain't goin' back. Don't matter what you say. Done made up my mind. Them fellers I kilt deserved what they got. Wouldn't't've chopped 'em up lessen they went and done something what warranted it. Bastards cheated me."

Thought to continue my partner's method and reason with the murderous skunk. "We don't care why you killed 'em. You can tell your story to Judge Pedigrew in Fort Worth, Twiggens. He's a good man and puts on a fair trial," I said.

My partner raised a quieting hand as if to motion me into silence. Given the gift of time and hindsight, guess I should have kept my mouth shut. What little I could see of Twiggens's face behind his shovel-sized beard flushed up. Deep-set eyes almost crossed and went all wild-looking.

"Done tole you more'n once, goddammit. I ain't a-goin' back, by God," the creature growled. "You fellers both deef, stupid, or

19

somethin'?"

Boz moved his soothing hand up as though to shush our angry killer. "Don't go and get yourself all riled up now, Dolphus," he said.

"You go straight to a burning Hell, Tatum. Done made up my mind. Git riled up any damned time I feel the urge, by God. Ain't lettin' no man string me up to a crossbeam and watch me mess my pants in front of a bunch of whiskey-saturated Saturday afternoon gawkers. You boys is gonna have to kill me right here."

And then, Sweet Merciful Jesus, before I could blink twice, that monstrous son of a bitch snatched up a double-bit ax from behind the doorframe, let out a screeching yelp that brought a branded panther to mind, took two steps, jumped, and flew at us like some kind of gigantic bird. Flapped his arms like he actually thought he could fly. Swear to God, his face turned into a skeletal mask that looked exactly like Death's very own self. Lord have mercy, scared the burning, sulfurous hell out of me.

In mid-flight, he brought that ax down right in the middle of Sunset's head. Poor beast's skull split like a ripe melon. Blood sprayed in forty directions at the same instant. Splattered all over me, Boz, and everything within fifteen feet of where we sat them animals. Horse never made a sound. Dropped like a felled tree with Twiggens on top, clawing his way toward my stunned friend, who had gone and got tangled up in his stirrups.

All the screaming, jumping, and blood caused Grizz to crow-hop sideways. He humped up, bucked, and deposited me on the porch. Flimsy, near-rotten, rough-cut boards collapsed when I landed. Went through on my back and hit hard. Cloud of dust and splinters fell all over me. Then the poor crazed beast headed any place away from the brutally bloody action. Took some seconds to scramble out of the pile of busted-up timber and rusted nails.

Finally staggered to unsteady feet, just in time to see that Twiggens had Boz by the throat and held him in the air like a child's corn-shuck doll. He rattled ole Boz, from head to foot, as easy as any whiskey slinger waves a wet bar rag at spilled booze on a busy Saturday night in Hell's Half Acre.

Figured out right quick my shotgun was about as worthless as a nail without a hammer. Would've killed both of them had I fired. Pitched the sawed-off aside, and pulled two pistols about the time Boz fumbled around and managed to get a grip on his short-barreled belly gun. He brought it up between the two of them and pushed the muzzle against his attacker's breastbone.

Barely heard the muffled blast from the Colt when it went off. Two shots knocked Twiggens backward and forced his fingers from around Boz's neck. Both slugs came out of the big man's back in separate wads of tissue, bone, and a vaporous cloud of bloody spray.

My friend's brutal method had the desired effect. Ole Dolphus dropped to his knees, coughed, spit, and clawed at his throat like he had a fistful of cockleburs stuck somewhere behind raw tonsils and couldn't cough them up.

He knee-walked a step or two, landed on his perforated back like an anvil dropped from Heaven. Stunned the hell out of me when he did a rubber ball and bounced right back up on wobbly legs like nothing had happened. Grabbed at the two holes in his chest, and let out a shriek that made my eyes water.

Then, I swear before Jesus, he bent over and puked gouts of blood, bone, and everything he'd eaten in a week. Straightened up, and shot a murderous glance my direction. Stumbled toward me with one arm out like a blind drunk searching for a hidden bottle of Old Spider Killer. Tripped over poor Sunset's gore-drenched neck, fell, and hopped up again. A blood-saturated hand the size of a camp skillet covered holes in his chest that oozed and bubbled a crimson froth.

Have to admit, I found myself in something of a state of flabbergastedness. Hell, I'd never witnessed anything to match it. Stood like a tree rooted since the beginning of recorded time. Couldn't believe a man as dead as the twice-shot Dolphus Twiggens could still suck air and move around. But by God he could, and headed for me with the look of death on an ashen skull of a face and murder in his flat black eyes.

Must have finally come back to myself when he was almost on top of me. Would wager I ripped off half a dozen shots fast as I could thumb them. Got him dead center with every single one of those bullets, but he kept coming. Dead man stumbled one final step, and fell on me like a downtown Dallas brick bank building. Damn near crushed the life out of me — right on the spot.

Not sure how long I laid there and tried to push that gushing three-hundred-pound corpse off. Couldn't breathe worth a bucket of cold spit. Then, of a sudden, the weight rolled away, and Boz jerked me up by the collar. Helped me over to the porch and made me sit. Slapped me on the back till I thought my eyes would pop out. Had me bend over at the waist and take in as much air as I could. Got all my innards started back up again.

Then he stomped over to the corpse and went to talking to it. "Hope you like the way everything turned out, you crazy bastard. Just couldn't go peaceable, could you? Just had to fight. Made up your feeble-assed mind not to get hung. Settled on gettin' shot all to hell and gone. And on top of everything else, you killed my horse, you son of a bitch."

For a few seconds I went to thinking as how maybe my friend and mentor had completely lost his mind. He finally did come back around to something like sanity. But that was only after he'd pulled his hip pistol and plugged ole Dolphus three more times. Said it was just to make sure, you know.

Suppose the worst part of the whole affair was the burying of that monster. Found some rusted shovels in the corral. Took both of us the better part of half a day to dig a hole big enough for his moose-sized corpse.

Had to run Grizz down. Looped a rope around Twiggens's feet, and dragged him into the grave. Otherwise, we never would have got him underground.

Boz threw the last shovelful of dirt on the grave, ripped his hat off, held it over his heart. Thought, Jesus, is he going to offer up a prayer for ole Dolphus?

He got right thoughtful-looking and said, "Dear sweet God, please don't let this son of a bitch get up again. I'm tired of shootin' 'im. Amen."

Took both of us a spell to get over the events of that fateful afternoon. Just nothing like blood, gore, and a near-death experience to send a man to his prayers at night. Had absolutely no doubt in my mind that I'd seen the true face of Death that day for real and awful. Had to mention it when I spoke with God that night.

'Course those feelings only stayed with me for about two months. That's when me and Boz rode into a pissant-sized town named Salt Valley in search of a spot to lock Buster Caldwell up for a spell. Salt Valley's where I *truly* saw Death for the very first time. Soul-stealing bastard crept up on me unawares, as it were. He's snaky like that, you know. Get to you when you least expect it. I've never forgotten what he looks like, or

the black-haired angel a benevolent God
sent to save me from his icy clutches.

1

"WHO CARES 'BOUT DIRTY-LEGGED WHORES?"

Buster Caldwell, a cowboy from down San Antone way, got liquored up over in Hell's Half Acre one night, and decided he couldn't live another second without the attentions of a ruby-lipped, fancy woman. Hoofed it over to Mattie Osborn's parlor house on Rusk Street, and picked a cute little buck-toothed gal named Goldie Starr for the ride. Fellers called her Goldie 'cause one of them squirrel-like teeth of hers was as gold as could be and sparkled like a star in the night sky when she smiled.

Stories, rumors, and outright lies followed his deadly visit. Truth is, no one knows for sure exactly what happened after Buster closed the door to Goldie's room. But about twenty minutes into their whoop-and-holler session, that horny brush popper went crazier than a feather mattress full of bedbugs. For reasons beyond all human understanding, he pulled a nine-inch bowie knife and damned nigh sawed that poor girl's head clean off.

Folks swore you could hear little Goldie scream bloody murder a quarter of a mile away and above all the racket typical of a Saturday night in the Acre. Leastways till he sliced through her windpipe, that is. One man I talked with, who was waiting his turn out in the parlor, tried to help the murdered girl. He testified as how the only thing that kept the corpse's head attached to its body was the neck bone.

Captain Wag Culpepper called me and my partner, Boz Tatum, into Company B's headquarters tent the following morning, shook his stubby finger in our faces, and said, "It's bad enough that every other cow-punchin' leather pounder between here and the Rio Grande counts himself as a badman and looks to prove it at the first opportunity. Sons of bitches will fight each other with guns, knives, barrel staves, fence posts, and whiskey bottles at the drop of a palm-leaf sombrero. Now we've got a woman killer runnin' loose. Poor workin' girls have a miserable enough time makin' a livin' as it is. Women shouldn't have to worry about being brutally cut into several different gruesome pieces by one of their idiot clients."

Boz assumed a sagelike, chin-stroking pose, nodded, and said, "Absolutely, Cap'n. Damned right. Couldn't agree more. Me and Lucius feel exactly the same way, by God. We'll get 'im and see justice is done. Bring ole Buster back to hang. Cain't have such ignorant brutality runnin' amuck right here in town like this."

Culpepper, furrowed lines of concern etched into a haggard face, heaved his bulk out of a dilapidated camp chair, and moved around to our side of a Civil War campaign table, dented and scarred by time and heavy use.

He clapped iron-fingered hands on my shoulder and Boz's. "Know you boys won't ever mention it to my wife, but Mattie Osborn's an old friend. We go way back. All the way to the time before Fort Worth amounted to much more'n a bump in the west Texas wind. You're the best men I've got. Never fail to do whatever's necessary. Know you'll bring Caldwell back, if you can, or kill him, if you have to. Whichever way it falls out, want you to find the murderin' skunk, and make sure he don't never kill another woman."

'Course, we promised we would. Chased Caldwell through the briars and brambles all around Abilene. Running gun battle that covered every foot of five miles developed once we finally spotted him. Hunt ended when we cornered his sorry self in a stand of timber along a rugged, unnamed, snag-filled arroyo, a bit south of the Colorado River. Efforts at persuading the murdering skunk to consider surrender, with an abundance of hot lead and heated threats, failed. Buster wasn't havin' none of it.

He'd managed to hide behind an enormous fallen cottonwood lodged in the creek bank after his horse pulled up lame. Burrowed himself in like an Alabama tick and yelled, "You fellers best go on back to Fort Worth. Swear I'll kill anyone what gets too close. 'Specially you law-bringin' Ranger sons of bitches."

Threw out a thick blanket and got comfortable. Laid on my back behind a sizable chunk of rock, and rolled myself a smoke. Pitched a shot or two over my shoulder every so often, just to give ole Buster something to think about. Boz did his best Comanche tiptoe to flank the murderin' weasel.

Took a puff, blew a nice smoke ring toward heaven, and yelled back, "Might as well give it up, Buster. We don't want to kill you, you son of a bitch, but we will if you force it."

Dolphus Twiggens still occupied a blood-saturated spot in my mind, but from all I'd seen, Caldwell appeared less than half that horse killer's size. And besides, he couldn't shoot worth a sack full of horse apples.

Sounded mighty nervous when he yelped, "Ain't afeard of you Ranger bastards. Don't mean nothin' to me. Kill your sorry asses as quick as any other man. Come on in here and git some, if'n you've got the *cojones.*"

Like a graveyard-haunting ghost, Boz had vanished into the thickets. I knew he'd be on Buster like ugly on an armadillo so fast the poor waddie wouldn't know what happened. Tatum had all the most deadly qualities of a combination Comanche, rattlesnake, and panther once he got on a badman's odiferous scent.

Figured it best to keep our quarry's attention. Wanted to draw him back my direction when I said, "Not after you for killin' men, Buster. You went and tried to cut that poor Goldie Starr's head clean off in the Acre. Still call that murder here in Texas. Gotta take you back to Fort Worth. You're gonna hang for that 'un."

Sounded upset, red-faced, and slobbery when he hollered back, "Hell, she warn't nothin' more'n a dirty-legged whore, Ranger. Who cares 'bout dirty-legged whores? Probably done the world a favor when I kilt that diseased bitch."

"Me and Boz Tatum care, Buster. State of Texas, Texas Rangers, and the good citizens of Fort Worth."

"Horseshit. Cain't believe anyone'd actually arrest and hang me for an act that borders on true community service. Way I've got it figured, a man should be on salary for such beneficial efforts on behalf of the public's health and welfare."

Sad to say it, but Buster's brutal assessment of the demimonde's situation in the Acre amounted to a fairly accurate appraisal of how most of the drovers traveling north to the Kansas railheads felt on the subject. Abuse and death proved ever-present companions for those poor women desperate enough to enter a wickedly violent and degrading life. Facts of the time were undeniable that far too many of those who passed on unexpectedly went out by means similar to those credited to Caldwell. Sizable number died at the hand of some poor, drunken, south Texas cow chaser. Really sad way to live. And die.

Even worse, a good deal of the time, despondent unfortunates took their own lives — usually after years of mistreatment, alcoholism, opium addiction, and horrendously debilitating health problems. Sad and unpleasant to think on it, but none of that gave anyone the right to do what Buster'd done. I've always believed murder's murder, no matter how you slice it. Last I heard, attempting to cut a woman's head off still qualified.

And as Randall Bozworth Tatum always said, "Hanging is the perfect punishment for any man who'd abuse or viciously kill a woman. Got not one grain of sympathy for such animals. I'd ride a hundred miles to watch a woman killer drop through the trap and swing. Buy me an ear of flame-roasted corn on the cob and applaud when he hit the end of the rope and messed hisself. Yessir, as fine an afternoon's entertainment as I could conjure up after a week of thinkin' on the subject."

Couldn't have taken more'n a puff or three off my cigareet when I heard several quick shots and considerable pained screaming from Buster's direction. Then Boz yelled out, "Come on in, Lucius. Done tamed this mad dog a bit. Don't think he's got any bite left."

Hopped down the creek bank and slogged through knee-deep trash and snag-filled water to Caldwell's muddy hidey-hole. With a still-smoking pistol in each hand, Boz stood over the poor stupid gomer and shook his head as I climbed up on a comfortable log and took a seat.

Wounded cowboy rolled around behind the dead tree in a deer wallow. Cowardly stink sprayer whimpered and cried like a little girl. With both hands, he clasped an oozing hole in his left side just above the waistband of his filthy trousers. Goodly amount of blood already saturated most of an equally nasty shirt's tail, and some even soaked into his pistol belt.

"Aw, shut the hell up," Boz snapped. "Big ole slug went in and came right out. Didn't hit nuthin' real important. If'n I'd of blasted through a piece of gut or somethin', I could understand all this bawlin' and carryin' on. But Hell's eternal fire, I didn't do nothin' 'cept punch a hole in that 'ere fleshy part just above your cartridge belt. Ain't gettin' no sympathy here. Whining skunks like you make me wanna heave up my spurs." He holstered one pistol and set to reloading the other.

"Damn your back-shootin' soul, it hurts like Hell's own blazes," Buster whimpered. "Look at this mess you went and done to me. I could, by God, bleed to death right here in this deer waller. Wound might well get all festerated. Might cause me to die from bad blood. Seen it happen out on the trail a number of times. Horrible way to go out — screamin' and pukin' and such. Jesus, help me. Sweet Jesus, come and help poor Buster."

Boz grinned, holstered his reloaded pistol, and said, "Yeah, and you could get hit by lightning too, you woman-killin' son of a bitch. Sizzle like a jackrabbit on a spit. And by the way, callin' on the Deity ain't gonna help you none, for certain sure. Only thing between you and eternity is me and Lucius Dodge."

"You boys gotta get me to a doc. Gotta do it quicklike." Caldwell whimpered like a kicked dog, sounded panicky, and looked like a man about to pass out. And, hell, then he did. Fluttering eyes rolled up in his head. He flopped over on his side like a beached catfish, and went to puking all over hell and yonder.

"We could run him to Salt Valley," I said. "Ain't but maybe twenty-five, thirty miles from here as the crow flies. Heard tell as how they's a fair enough pill roller in residence over that way. Throw this sack of manure in a cell, and get him patched up. Leave 'im there till we feel like takin' 'im back to Fort Worth."

Boz stared down at Caldwell, crinkled his

nose, and shook his head in disgust. "Wouldn't hurt my feelings one bit if the worthless son of a bitch bled out right where he's laying, Lucius. Muddy deer waller is a good 'nuff spot for his departure from this life, as far as I'm concerned. Be a better way and place to go out than he gave poor little Goldie Starr." Hard to argue with such reasoning. Then again, we both knew we'd have to do something.

Continued to urge my partner in the right direction. He could be real hardheaded when he wanted. I said, "Don't know about you, Boz, but I'd like to sleep in a bed for a night or two. We've been living on the ground so long I'm beginning to grow a crop of wildflowers between my toes. Know how much you love snoozin' under an open sky, but I need a real bath, an actual meal cooked by someone other than you, and a bottle of giggle juice. We could rest up a few days, then drag ole Buster back to civilization for suitable trial and hanging."

Took about five seconds, but Boz smiled and dropped his angry stance. He scratched a stubbly whisker-covered chin. "Well, could use a bath, shave, and I'm just as tired of my cooking as you are. Hell, let's do 'er. We'll put a travois together and drag his sorry little ass to Salt Valley."

36

"You know the local law there, Boz?"

"Yeah. Town marshal's an old friend. Name's Caleb Oakley. Fine feller. Used to Ranger with me down on the border around Reynosa a few years back."

"Well, let's get at it. Put on some speed and we could be back to civilization in a couple of hours."

Got Buster loaded onto a pole drag, and on our way in pretty short order. Brought his poor limpin' buckskin cayuse along as well. Pulled into Salt Valley 'bout an hour or so past noon.

Bustling village had the typical appearance of most small Texas towns of the 1880s. Sliced by two or three lesser east-to-west avenues, a single north-to-south through street ran for about two hundred yards before petering out on the north end of town. Lined on either side by a variety of clapboard buildings. The village fathers had actually planted trees at precise intervals along the main thoroughfare. Town buzzed with farmers and ranchers, and was a more-than-welcome sight.

Stopped in front of the marshal's office and jail. Boz said, "I'll take care of this, Lucius. Why don't you head on over to the Holy Moses Saloon and Restaurant yonder. Corner a table. Order us up a steak dinner and a bottle."

Sounded like a fine plan to me. Nodded my agreement, and eased Grizz back across the main thoroughfare. Climbed down and tied him to the hitch rail out front of what appeared to be Salt Valley's premier liquor-pouring and eating establishment. Heavy plate-glass window revealed a glistening bar and cloth-covered tables decorated with picked flowers and real silverware. Couldn't help but shake my head in amused wonderment.

Used my hat to slap as much dust off myself as I could. Must have resembled a living dirt devil there for a spell. Grit swirled around as I tried to dance my way out of the grimy cloud.

Started for the combination saloon–restaurant's batwing doors. Had my hand on top of one of them when thunderous gunfire, three or four doors down the boardwalk, got my attention. Commotion inside the Farmer's and Rancher's Bank sent folks out in the street scurrying in every direction. Women screamed. Horses nearest the action went into a panic.

'Bout the time I pulled my pistols, two fellers wearing bandannas over their faces busted through the bank's fancy, carved-mahogany and glass double doors. Both men carried stuffed bags in one hand, pistols in the other, and headed for animals tied out front.

Thieves set to blazing away at anything they could see that moved. First thing they hit was a draft horse attached to a beer wagon. One of the wild-shooting bandits sent a skin-singeing slug across his haunches. Wounded beast let out a terrible shriek of pain and surprise. Animal bolted at breakneck speed and headed for parts unknown. Untethered beer barrels bounced out of the wagon's bed and flew all over the street.

Ducked behind the saloon's door frame. Tried to hide myself. Hadn't been there more'n a second or so when, from the corner of my eye, I spotted a woman and a small child in the middle of the street. They'd been unfortunate enough to be dead center of the roadway when all the indiscriminate blasting started, and had nowhere to run. Woman hunkered down and wrapped herself around the youngster like a living blanket. Their deadly plight spurred me into unthinking action.

Jumped into the thoroughfare. Ran directly toward the robbers and a sizzling wall of pistol fire. Got myself planted between the distressed lady and the shooters. Stupid jackasses couldn't get themselves horsed. Their skittish animals, spooked by all the noise and violent activity, danced and twirled as the panicked robbers continued to blaze away. Bullets flew around me like angry Mexican hornets.

Paused, took careful aim, and snapped off a round that drilled the tallest of the two stickup artists dead center as he tried to climb aboard his animal. Got him right where he was biggest. Shot knocked the gunman back to the ground. Appeared to me he probably saw the bottoms of his own boots on the way down. One foot got jammed up in a stirrup. Frightened pony dragged his limp body away.

Downed man's panic-stricken partner turned and thumbed off at least three rounds that zipped past my head and kicked up dirt near my feet. He exhausted one weapon, shoved it into a hip holster, then went for his belly gun.

I took a few more steps in the thief's direction. Was about to unload on him from both smoke wagons when a third brigand jumped through the bank's open doors. Ripped off a shot that knocked my hat into the air. Hot lead burned a deep crease just above my ear.

Of a sudden, most of the color went out

of the world. Felt like I'd been hit in the head with a long-handled shovel. Grabbed at the bloody crease, went to my knees, and rolled onto my back. Both shooters had me in their sights by then. Hot slugs pounded the ground all around me while I rolled in the dirt. Remember thinking as how they'd have the range soon enough.

My eyes didn't want to work right. Everything I could still see turned a murky mix of red, gray, and black. Held my blood-covered hand up in front of my face, but couldn't count the fingers. Could hear people yelling, but the words didn't make no sense. Got this taste in my mouth like I'd been sucking on a copper penny freshly dug up after years in the ground.

Then, as God is my witness, just before much-desired unconsciousness reached up and jerked me into a sticky, red pit, a black-haired angel, dressed in white, appeared by my side. She held the hand of a pink-cheeked, cherub-faced child. Her skirts billowed out on the hot breezes as she bent over me.

The youngster touched me on the forehead and said, "Don't worry, mister, my mommy will save you."

Time turned into something like molasses in January, but I swear 'fore Jesus the

41

woman said, "Give me your pistol, sir."

She took one of the weapons from my unfeeling hand, stood, turned sidewise like a New Orleans-trained duelist, and fired, at least twice, before I completely blacked out. God reached down and tipped me into a hole so deep, it felt like I'd never be able to crawl out. Could still hear shots being fired when the blackness claimed me body and soul.

2

". . . THERE'S GONNA BE HELL TO PAY . . ."

Clawed my muddy-headed way back from the other side, and found myself stretched out on a lumpy cot in one of Marshal Caleb Oakley's spartan jail cells. Boz sat next to me in a straight-backed, cane-bottomed chair. Wafting smoke from his well-chewed panatela smelled mighty good. He noticed my eyes had opened. The tougher-than-boot-heels Ranger smiled, leaned over, and offered me a sip of water from a tin dipper he pulled out of a wooden bucket.

"Feeling better there, pard? You've been gone between thirty minutes and an hour. Knew you weren't all that bad off. Seen you get hurt a helluva lot worse at least a dozen times."

As I sipped from the dipper, heard Buster Caldwell grumble from somewhere, "Wuz hopin' the son of a bitch had died myself. Wish all you Rangers a blood-spittin' departure, and an early welcome in Satan's fiery pit, by God."

Boz glanced to a spot somewhere over the top of my head and snapped, "Shut your stupid mouth, Buster. You may be wounded and locked up, but that won't keep me from comin' in there and stompin' a ditch in your sorry woman-killin' backside."

Coughed, and fingered the bandage on my head. "How'd that dance in the street finally play out?"

He ignored my question. "Local doc says you've got a nice new groove in your skull bone there, Lucius. Said not to mess with the dressing for a day or so. Best heed the man's warnin' and stop fingerin' around on it. Wouldn't want to start you bleedin' again."

"My ears are still ringing like chapel bells in a Mexican church. Suppose maybe I should consider myself lucky." Kept picking at the bandage.

Boz reached over and pulled my hand away from the swath of crusted gauze. "Well, you're a sight better off than them bank robbers. Two of them boys got sent to Jesus for His immediate attention. One feller's wounded. He'll live on. You put a slug in his side a little below his gun belt. Bullet came out his left buttock." He snickered and added, "Feller ain't gonna sit a

horse anytime soon and goin' to the outhouse is gonna be a totally new experience."

Mumbled, "Knew I hit at least one feller.
Seen his horse drag him away. One of them
boys musta got lucky." Of a sudden I re-
membered the woman. "Strangest thing
happened just 'fore I passed out, Boz. Who
killed that other one?"

Boz shook his head. Thumped ashes from
his smoke onto the floor. "Hard to fathom,
but that 'un as you shot came loose from
his pony and managed to stand. And you
ain't gonna come nowhere toward believin'
what happened next."

"Black-haired angel in a white dress
stepped in?"

"How'd you know that?"

"Saw her before I went under. Leastways,
thought I saw her. Figure from your response she was real — weren't she?"

"Oh, she was real enough. Hope to God I
don't ever have to get into a lead-pitchin'
contest with that particular woman. Gal can
handle a pistol like John Wesley Hardin on
his best day. Let me get Caleb. Have him
tell you all about the lady. Old lawman's
well acquainted with her."

He patted me on the shoulder, stood, and
jingled his way back to the jail's outer office. Heard voices but, once again, couldn't

45

tell what got said. Came to think as how the head wound had affected my hearing some. Still couldn't see right either. Had strange, odd-shaped, floating spots behind my eyes that created vision gaps. Made concentration an effort.

Guess I must have drifted off. Came back again when a feller with a face like a chewed-leather saddlebag, and sporting a droopy white moustache, gently shook my arm. He cast a grandfatherly smile my direction, sat in Boz's recently vacated chair, and appeared to gaze down at me with something akin to genuine concern.

"Right sorry you got hurt, young feller." Marshal Caleb Oakley's deep baritone voice went miles toward solidifying an almost godlike appearance. "This kind of gunplay just don't happen in Salt Valley very often. In fact, today's the first time such deadly events have transpired since I took over as marshal. This here's my town, and it's usually a peaceful little place."

Tried to lean up on one uncooperative elbow, but dizziness and creeping nausea put me on my back in a hurry. Held a trembling hand over my sweat-covered brow and said, "Boz tells me you know the fine-shooting lady who stepped up and saved me, Marshal."

"Not well, but I do know who she is. Must admit I didn't have no idea she could put on a shootin' display the likes of what folks witnessed in the street today, though." He cut his answer short. Didn't seem inclined to go any further unless prodded.

"Any possibility you could tell me her name? Would like very much to thank her when I'm up and about. Maybe send a note, if I'm not able to do the deed in person."

"Name's Dianna Savage. Mrs. Dianna Savage. She and the child showed up in town 'bout a year back. One thing everyone seems privy to about Mrs. Savage is that she doesn't appear to need for anything in the way of money. Bought a house and right fine piece of property out on the far north edge of town, 'bout a mile from the sawmill. Paid every penny in cash to banker Hiram King. Keeps pretty much to herself. Nothing as I've witnessed in her past demeanor would have indicated a capability for what transpired out in the street today."

"So, take it she has a husband around someplace?"

"Not as I, or anyone else, know of. Story most of the womenfolk around town tell, over their weekly washing, is that her man got his sad self killed when a horse fell on him year or so 'fore she settled in these parts. Most tend to believe she came to us from over near Waco, but ain't no one makin' any serious coin bettin' on that particular piece of information. Being a seriously private person, she ain't sayin' one way or t'other."

"Ah. Well, I'll make it a point to stroll by and express my heartfelt thanks quick as I can get off this cot and out of your cell."

Oakley got right thoughtful-looking. Slowly ran a hand through his iron-gray hair. "Don't mean to throw water on your thinkin', but there might be a small problem with your plans, son."

"What kind of problem?" I asked.

"Appears one of the fellers Mrs. Savage blasted to Kingdom Come, whilst in the process of savin' your valuable hide, was none other than the infamous west Texas badman Reuben Coffin."

The name dropped between us like a rancid corpse. Every Ranger in Texas worth his salt had heard something awful about the light-fingered and lethal Coffin brothers. Most notable of the deadly pair of ruffians was a hard-eyed killer named Nate. All of a sudden, and on top of the throbbing ache from my newly acquired skull decoration, a piercing pain like an ice pick speared through a spot somewhere behind my right eye.

Rubbed my throbbing temple and said, "Not thinking straight, Marshal. Did you just say that Mrs. Savage killed Nate Coffin's worthless brother?"

"Baby brother, as a pure matter of absolute fact. Loved by everyone in their extensive family — including a cadre of aunts, uncles, and soft-brained cousins who live in, and around, Carrizo Springs. Way I've got it figured, the straight-shootin' Mrs. Savage has about three weeks left amongst the living once Nate Coffin finds out what happened here in Salt Valley today."

Rolled onto my back and moaned. Used a heavy arm to shield my eyes from the sunlight pouring through a barred window above the cot. Mumbled, "Thought Nate Coffin and his boys pretty much worked the area around Uvalde, Del Rio, and Eagle Pass. Last I heard, Nate killed a couple of cowboys over close to Crystal City 'cause they insulted his hat."

"Hadn't heard that 'un, but it wouldn't surprise me none. Must be at least fifty gruesome and gory stories goin' 'round 'bout how he's killed the hell out of a boatload of innocents for a lot less in the way of provocation."

Peeked at him from beneath my shirtsleeve. "You truly believe Coffin would show up here and murder Mrs. Savage?"

Man shook his head like a tired dog. "Way news travels these days, and especially news like that of a woman killing no less than Reuben Coffin in a stand-up gunfight, no doubt about it. Tale of this shooting will be all over Hell and Texas inside a week. Figure Mrs. Savage will be under the ground 'fore the month's out. And I'll probably go in a grave right beside her when I try to stop the inevitable." Oakley leaned forward and propped his head in his hands. "Lady mighta saved your life today, Lucius. But there's gonna be hell to pay for how she went about it."

Fought off the dizziness, forced myself upright, and swung my legs over the edge of the cot. Reached out and placed my hand on the old marshal's sagging shoulder. Boz appeared at the cell door with a fresh cup of coffee in one hand and his unfinished panatela in the other.

I said, "Long as I'm living, Caleb, you and Mrs. Savage are safe as newborn babes. Swear on my father's grave, if any of the Coffin family shows up, they'll have to kill me to get to either of you."

Boz laughed, then said, "Same here. I've

had a run-in or two with the elder Coffin some years ago. Murderous rogue is still carryin' a chunk of my lead. He don't scare me none."

Felt some better the next morning when Boz shook me awake and handed me a big plate of scrambled eggs, a slab of ham, and a fine-smelling cup of Marshal Oakley's special belly wash. Sat them on a stool near the bed and tried to eat a bit. But the ache in the side of my head left me to sip at the cup more than anything else.

"How's that ironbound noggin of yours, boy?"

Gingerly checked out the bandage-covered wrinkle over my ear with the tips of trembling fingers. "Well, it has stopped bleeding. Seems a mite improved. Don't hurt near like it did yesterday. Leastways, not yet. Might want to check back in about two hours. Should be throbbin' pretty good by then."

Surprised me more'n a little when my partner shot me a conspiratorial smile, leaned over, and whispered, "Someone special here to see you, Lucius. Think you're gonna be right pleased with this particular visitor."

He stepped aside, and there stood the stunning Dianna Savage. My God but she was a beauty. Tall, narrow-waisted, ample-bosomed, full-hipped, black hair done in a fashionable, upswept bun. Unblemished complexion and the naturally reddest lips I'd ever seen on a woman. Made a mental note as how my eye-catching guest bore a striking resemblance to a heavenly being portrayed in a painting that hung in the foyer of the Tarrant County Court House. Picture was a portrayal of a winged seraph leading small children over a fast-running creek in a dense forest. Amazing image had the power to stop me dead in my tracks for a viewing every time I passed it. Tried to stand and act the gentleman.

"Please don't trouble yourself, sir," Mrs. Savage said, and waved me back to my seat on the cot.

"Thank you. I'm still a mite fuzzy-headed today."

No reluctance or hesitation. She boldly stepped forward and offered her hand. The lady had a cool, firm grip. "I am most pleased to see you're doing somewhat better, Mr. Dodge. Given the way you looked a few moments after we first met, I had my doubts you'd enjoy another day amongst the living."

"My sentiments exactly, Mrs. Savage. Please tell me, is your child safe and well?"

"Yes indeed, sir. My son's well-being is the precise reason for my hasty and unannounced visit this morning. I came to offer my sincerest thanks for your efforts at saving us from those killers. Had you not stepped up to the situation, and bodily placed yourself at peril between us and them, I am convinced William and I would have surely died in the dust of Main Street during yesterday's bloody altercation."

A crystalline tear rolled down her flawless cheek. She dabbed at it with a small white kerchief and, though racked with emotion, did a curtsy that slowly turned into a royally regal and well-practiced bow. Her chin touched her chest as she almost whispered, "I am eternally in you debt, Ranger Dodge."

Stunned, flattered, and somewhat embarrassed by such a display, I motioned for her to rise. Eventually her head came up and she gazed into my eyes. "Please, Mrs. Savage, I'm the one who should be thanking you. If my muddled memory serves, you reciprocated my feeble efforts and came to my aid at a most opportune instance. And if what Ranger Tatum and Marshal Oakley tell me is even close to the truth, your courageous conduct during the previous day's attempted robbery bordered on the astonishing."

She blushed. Her chin dropped back to an ample and well-proportioned bosom, then came up again. I could barely see liquid turquoise eyes as she said, "I took the action necessary at the time, sir. I blame my impetuousness on a father who trained me to fight the vicious Comanche at an extremely early age. Brock Armstrong had no patience with shirkers, or those unwilling to defend themselves when the necessity came. By the time of my tenth birthday, I could fire a pistol, and rifle, as well as any man settled along the Balcones Escarpment west of San Antonio. But my actions would never have been possible but for your initial intervention."

Managed to get to my feet on still-unsteady legs. Reached out and took her hand again. Drew her out of the bow so I could look her straight in the face. "All that really matters, so far as I'm concerned, is that you and the boy survived unscathed, and that men bent on robbery and murder have met their Maker."

Released her fingers, and she immediately dipped into a small black bag that hung from one wrist. "My calling card, sir. Please present this at my door whenever you like. I would consider it an honor to, at the very least, provide the man who saved my child's life with a home-cooked meal prepared at his convenience." She curtsied again, turned, and, in a rush of wildly feminine sounds and smells, vanished through the jail's barred doorway into Marshal Oakley's office.

Held the card up to my nose and sniffed. "Ummm. Lilac."

Boz leaned against the cell door, snorted, and shook his head. "My, my, my," he said. "That's one helluva woman there, Lucius. If'n I was you, I'd be on the lady's doorstep this afternoon redeeming her card, for whatever it might be worth."

"Sweet weepin' Jesus, Boz. You should be ashamed of your randy old self for even thinking such low thoughts. Any man with one good eye and half a brain can see that Mrs. Dianna Savage is a well-bred lady of impeccable upbringing and flawless manners. Not one of those high-toned soiled doves from Hell's Half Acre you favor. On top of all that, I owe the lady more than I could possibly ever repay."

He held his hands up in mock distress as though to stop my verbal assault. "Didn't mean no offense there, pard. Merely an observation from an appreciative onlooker. Take it as you will. Besides, pretty sure I'd rather have a soiled dove that can't shoot quite as good as your lovely visitor."

Few days after Mrs. Savage's visit, Boz decided he'd go on ahead and escort Buster back to Fort Worth. While Caleb Oakley wasn't a man to complain, he let it be known that the town's fathers didn't care much for having to keep ole Buster in food and lodging for a crime he'd committed in another jurisdiction.

By the time Boz finally came to his decision, we'd taken a room in Salt Valley's only hotel, and my wounds had begun healing nicely. Must admit my equilibrium still suffered some at unexpected intervals, and hearing from my right ear proved problematic at times. Otherwise, I couldn't complain.

Stood in the street and shook my good friend's hand while he sat his horse. He said, "See to your health, Lucius. Come on along as you deem the time is right. Should anything go amiss, get word to me as quickly as possible and I'll come back straightaway. Make it a point to stop at the telegraph office daily and check for any messages from you. Don't hesitate to send a wire if you need help."

"You do the same, Boz. Keep a weather eye on Buster. Man knows what's waiting for him at the end of this ride. He's just the kind of sneak who'd try something unexpected and deadly. Should any of the Coffin clan show their faces, you'll be the first to hear the news."

Guess I'd about recuperated by a week or so after Boz departed. While still a topic of daily gossip and conversation on the streets, and in the shops and saloons of Salt Valley, the whole dustup had finally begun to fade from memory. I attributed the rapid decline in the tale's popular esteem to the fact that no locals had died or been wounded in the fight. Folks had begun to relax and get on with their lives, as most are wont to do.

But lo and behold, one afternoon, a well-known killer rode in, set the whole town's teeth on edge, and got everyone tensed up again good and quicklike.

3

"I AIN'T NEVER KILT NO WOMAN."

Had me a nicely shaded spot staked out on the veranda in front of the Cattleman's Hotel when Burton Skaggs rode past and headed for the marshal's office. Recognized him from a chance meeting over in San Augustine, a year or so before. Skaggs was widely known as a soulless thief and killer of the first water. Knew without doubt his unexpected appearance on the scene would cause citizens, right and left, to arm themselves and look for any reason to start shooting. Damned dangerous situation.

Early morning breeze drifted under the rough lodge's portico and belied the coming of a scorching midday and unbearable heat. Watched from the comfort of a well-used chair as Salt Valley's newest arrival slinked past, stopped, climbed off a run-out gelding, and tied the bay to a convenient hitch rail directly in front of Marshal Caleb Oakley's office. Man and animal both appeared tired right down to the bone.

Any experienced observer would have harbored no doubt about the gunman's calling. Tall, rangy, dark, and sinister, Burton Skaggs looked the deadly part of man killer from heel to crown. Three pistols decorated a double-row cartridge belt strapped high around his narrow waist. A short-barreled shotgun rested in bindings behind a California saddle, and a massive Winchester hunting rifle filled an upright, easy-to-access boot in front.

He disappeared through the dark entrance of the marshal's office, but couldn't have been inside Oakley's headquarters more than a minute when both men gingerly stepped back onto the boardwalk. Watched as the old lawman pointed my direction, then led the gun for hire toward the hotel. Shifted my weight around to allow easy access to my hip pistol. Pulled my belly gun, cocked, and hid it beneath the week-old newspaper in my lap as well. Given recent events, along with an instant rash of chicken flesh up and down my back, felt fairly certain of another burst of gunfire in pretty short order.

Caleb motioned Skaggs to a stop on the step below my table and chair. "Mornin', Lucius. I trust you passed a comfortable night in one of the hotel's more restful beds?"

"That I did, Marshal Oakley, and thank you for asking. The Cattleman's mattresses do tend toward a degree more ease on a battered body than the hay-filled pallets in your jail cells."

"True, very true. This here's Burton Skaggs, Lucius." Caleb turned and made a halfhearted motion toward his companion. Gunman looked even more ferocious up close. Flat, slate-gray eyes bored into mine and gave the impression of absolute, bone-chilling fearlessness.

"I know who he is, Caleb. Our paths crossed briefly over in the Redlands a while back. Bet there's probably not a handful of Rangers in Texas who aren't familiar with the well-known, and deadly, Mr. Skaggs."

"He's just now arrived in town. Came by my office and asked if he could talk with you, first shot out of the box. That okay with you?"

Skaggs, thumbs hooked over his gun belt on either side of a heavy silver buckle, took a self-assured step away from Oakley's sheltering figure and growled, "Mean no malice toward you, Ranger Dodge. Or toward any of the other residents of Salt Valley during my visit today. Come bearin' news from the south I think will be of considerable interest, sir."

"Now, exactly what news could you possibly have from the south that I'd care one whit about, Skaggs?"

He sneered at my slight. Removed his flat-brimmed Stetson and wiped the sweaty inside with a ragged bandanna. As he carefully, and ceremoniously, replaced the hat, the gunman said, "Damn nigh rode a good horse to death gettin' here, Dodge. Least you could do is invite me to sit in the shade and talk a spell. Sure could use something to eat and a cool drink. Have my personal guarantee as how you absolutely do want to hear what I've got to say."

We glared at each other for about five more seconds before I nodded him to one of the two empty chairs at my table. He pushed Caleb aside, clomped up the steps, and dropped into the proffered seat like a man exhausted.

"You want me to stay on for a spell, Lucius?" Caleb asked. Could readily tell he lacked anything like a reasonable comfort level with Skaggs's ominous presence in his town.

Didn't take long to consider the marshal's concerned offer. Snatched a quick glance at the killer across the table from me. An almost imperceptible movement of his eyes sent an easily understandable message.

"No, Marshal. Do appreciate the offer, but think our guest and I'll get along just fine. You might do me a further service, though. Would you go inside and order up a drover's breakfast for Mr. Skaggs while we sit and talk? I'd be most grateful for the gesture."

Could tell from his expression Oakley balked at what he considered a crude dismissal. He threw me a pointed look, pushed his pistol butt forward with one hand, and scratched at a stubble-covered chin with the other.

"All right," he said. "Why don't you fellers just relax and take in Salt Valley's sweet-smelling morning air. I'll have a plate of victuals and something cold to drink sent out for you, Skaggs."

Soon as my new friend disappeared into the hotel's lobby, the flint-eyed gunny leaned forward in his chair, and fixed me with a case-hardened gaze. "Came to tell you that exactly a week ago Nate Coffin put out word as how he's willing to pay a handsome price for the head of a local woman what kilt his little brother."

"Seem to recollect as how you got jerked up short about a year ago for some kind of deadly fracas over around San Augustine, Skaggs."

If what I said fazed the man in the least, I couldn't tell it. He dismissed the question with the wave of his hand and said, "Simple misunderstanding. Already taken care of. You can wire the sheriff over that way, if'n you don't believe me."

Twisted in my chair and brought the newspaper up so the muzzle of my pistol was pointed directly at a spot about two inches above the gunhand's brightly polished belt buckle. Belly shot might not kill a man, but sure as hell hurts like the mortal dickens, and can render the strongest of them about as potent as a three-year-old suffering with the colic.

"Well, for now, I'll just have to trust you on that one, won't I? Any chance you're here to collect on Coffin's bounty?"

He flopped back into the chair, a look of total disgust on his face. Whipped off his hat and threw it into the only empty chair left at the table. Ran knotted fingers through sweaty hair and wagged his head back and forth. Threw a booted foot over one knee and played with the rowel on one of his spurs.

"Hell, no, Dodge. Came to warn you. Story 'bout what happened to Reuben Coffin's all over Hell and most of Texas. Killers for hire of every stripe already know about Nate's reward. Admit that I've done my share of sorry deeds over the years, but by God, every man has his limits. I ain't never kilt no woman. Shot a boy or two early on durin' the War of Yankee Aggression. But killin' women, or offering money to have one kilt, is beyond the pale as far as I'm concerned."

"How do you know all this, Skaggs? You certainly don't look like no crystal-ball gazer to me."

"Was down in Uvalde with Nate. Had my gun hired out to the man. When news of his little brother's untimely demise came, he went crazier'n a loco'd calf. Never seen anything like it."

"From what I've heard, Coffin's never been the most stable of God's creatures."

"Well, you're right about that 'un. Man's wilder'n a seal-tight full of sour kraut when nothing out of the ordinary, or beyond his control, transpires. But, by God, you let something like a beloved brother's brutal death occur and it's Katie-bar-the-door. Ain't nobody within two hundred miles of him safe right now."

"He's determined to kill someone then?"

"On my honor, sir, he's prepared to kill

everybody. Personally heard him say, 'Blood will have blood. The murderin' bitch responsible for Reuben's foul and untimely demise has got to die. I'll pay a thousand dollars in gold coin to any man who'll bring her back to me alive and kickin', or her head in a sack.' "

"Foul murder, you say? Reuben robbed Salt Valley's bank. Tried to kill me in the process. Came right near to succeedin'. Man got shot dead in a futile attempt to escape his own lawless behavior."

"Nate don't see it that way."

"Is that a natural fact? Big brother Nate must be an idiot, on top of everything else."

"Coffin's a lot of things, Dodge, but he ain't no idiot."

"You've an infamous reputation yourself, Skaggs. Why should I believe anything you've got to say on this particular subject? Could be you're lying through your teeth. Came here today to kill me as well."

A devilish smile spread across his rough-bearded, sunburned face. "All that could well be true. You'll have to believe as you see fit, Ranger. Either way, Mrs. Savage, as I believe the lady in question is called, is a walkin', talkin' female corpse. And you're right. That ain't the whole of it."

"What does that mean?"

"It means Nate Coffin put a price on you as well, Dodge. Figures you were the cause of the whole deadly incident by interfering with a legitimate, family-planned bank robbery, escape, and all. Says he'll pay twice as much for you as the woman, being as how you carry a reputation as a deadly adversary in a fight. If I wanted to make enough to live on for the next five years, all I'd have to do is kill you right now, then take care of the woman in my own sweet time."

Made certain my aim under the newspaper had him dead in his chair. "You might find such action a bit more difficult than you obviously now believe," I shot back.

"That could well be true too. But as I've already said, ain't come here with killin' in mind — you or the now-famous, straight-shootin' Mrs. Savage."

"That a fact?"

"Most certainly is. Just out to do a thoughtful, kindhearted, Christian deed for once in my benighted life. Rode day and night in service of that notion. Besides, don't matter what I do, or don't do. Every desperate, broke pistolero in Texas is gonna be after what they deem easy money, and they'll be arriving in Salt Valley mighty damned quick."

"You're absolutely certain?"

"Not a single doubt in my mind. Visit today is nothing more than a drop of water before a frog strangler of a spring cloudburst comin' your way. You and the lady are gonna go down chokin' on blood, if'n you don't heed my warnin'. Take some sincerely offered advice and get yourselves hid somewheres safe."

About then, Marshal Oakley led a white-shirted waiter who carried a tray of food out of the hotel. Piled with eggs, bacon, and biscuits, the three plates must have weighed near ten pounds. Our server delivered one heavily loaded dish to a spot in front of each chair, left, and quickly returned with a huge pitcher of ice-cold buttermilk.

Caleb handed Skaggs his hat and dropped into the open seat. "Hope you gents don't mind if I join you for breakfast. Don't know exactly what you've been jawin' about, but if it has anything to do with my town, or Mrs. Savage, I want to know."

Glanced at Skaggs for his approval, but would have said what I did without it. He nodded, and I went through his entire tale for the marshal's benefit. While I talked, the hungry gunfighter shoveled food in his face like a man filling up a grave. Went at the victuals with a speed and ferocity that reminded me of a hungry wolf out to devour a recent kill as quickly as possible so no other animal could get at it.

Oakley appeared not the least bit surprised by what he heard. When we finished, he laid his fork aside and said, "You gonna tell Mrs. Savage about this, or do you want me to do the job?"

No need for me to give that one much thought. "Lady offered to cook me a fine meal, Caleb. Guess I'll collect on her kind proposal this afternoon. See what we might be able to decide on in the way of preparation for Nate Coffin's revenge."

Oakley shot Skaggs a suspicious glance, then quickly turned back to me. "Be assured of my willingness to help in any way I can, Lucius. Skunks like this 'un don't scare me in the least."

Skaggs evidently chose to ignore Oakley's public chastisement. Sopped a biscuit through the leavings on his plate, cocked his head to one side, smiled like an idiot dog, and crammed the entire wad of bread into his mouth.

"Any way possible, Marshal, I'll get her out of town and back to Fort Worth," I said. "Surely Coffin isn't stupid enough to come right into Company B's headquarters after her."

With buttermilk, egg yolk, and a crop of

crumbs decorating his thick, drooping moustache, Skaggs gazed off at the farmers, ranchers, and tradesmen passing in the street. He shook his shaggy head and said, "Don't bet your life on it, Dodge. Nate Coffin is nefarious and unbelievably powerful. He'll send others, in the beginning. Feel you out. See if underlings can take care of the problem. If that don't work, trust me, he'll come hisself, kill every breathin' thing in this one-horse town, burn it to the ground, and scatter the ashes to the four winds. He's just that crazy — and a good bit more."

Bold statement really got Caleb's hackles up. Thought he'd jump across the table and slap the crumbs out of Skaggs's moustache when he snapped, "Such an eventuality could prove a great deal more difficult than you, or Coffin, believe, as long as I'm around and kickin', you mouthy son of a bitch."

Well, that ripped the rag off the bush. Second-rate assassin shook a finger in the marshal's face and growled, "Killin' an old fart like you ain't no chore for a big doer like me, Oakley. Best watch your words, old man."

Oakley's face went white. Figured I'd best jump in and stop the disagreement before the whole dance went too far. Held up a peacemaking hand between them, but kept my hidden weapon trained on the object of the marshal's ire.

Said, "Calm down, gents. Caleb, I'm sure our breakfast guest has no intention of staying on in Salt Valley any longer than necessary. Do you, Skaggs?"

He looked surprised at my assessment for about two seconds and shot back, "I'd like to get a bath and sleep in a bed, a night or two, before moving on."

"Why don't you do that," I suggested. "And as a gesture of my sincere appreciation for the information you've brought, let your short stay be my treat. Just tell the hotel desk clerk to put your room and bath on my bill."

My proposition had the desired effect. His attention moved from Caleb back to me. "Right nice of you to offer, Ranger Dodge, but I can take care of my own living expenses."

Nodded, waved, and said, "Whatever you want."

Angry gun hound shoved his chair away from the table and stood. "Well, what I say is, keep an eye peeled for other men like me. Heavily armed and with a dead-eyed look unlike any of the hoople-heads around these parts. Sure as chiggers itch, murderers are on their way as we speak. And be totally assured, they're comin' to kill you, and especially the woman, Dodge."

He eased around the table as though certain we meant to shoot him in the back. Disappeared into the hotel's lobby. Through the door, I heard him order up a room and steamin'-hot bath.

Caleb snatched his hat off and placed it in his lap. "Don't know about you, Dodge, but I believe 'im. Hard to admit such, but I do."

"Yeah, ugly tale definitely has the ring of truth. I'll get out to Mrs. Savage's place this afternoon. We'll work a plan and go from there."

Finished my breakfast. Strolled down the boardwalk and caught a freckle-faced kid in front of Broome's Mercantile and Dry Goods Store. Said, "You know where Mrs. Savage lives, son?"

"Yessir. Out on the north edge of town. End of Main Street. Past the sawmill."

"That's right. Give you four bits if you'll take this to her and wait for an answer."

On the back of Dianna Savage's calling card I wrote a short message inquiring if that evening would be convenient for her offer of a meal. Folded the tiny piece of paper, handed it to the kid, and said, "Wait

71

for her reply. You can find me over yonder on the hotel veranda, or maybe at the jail. Understand?"

"Where's my four bits?" he asked.

"Get it when you come back with my reply."

"Aw, come on, Ranger. You gotta cough up at least two bits, or I ain't doin' nothin'."

Must admit I admired the barefooted rascal's nerve. Paid him his two bits and he hit the road running. Thirty minutes later he found me back in my chair in the shade.

Snatched his hat off and held it against his chest with both hands. Said, "The lady wants me to say as how this afternoon around five o'clock would be mighty fine, if that's to your satisfaction. Said she would look forward to your visit, Ranger."

"That's just capital. Here's the rest of your money, young feller. Go back and tell her I'll be there."

He toed the dirt and shook his head. "Now I contracted to deliver your message fer four bits. You want another'n done, it'll cost you another four bits."

"Your daddy a lawyer by any chance?" I asked.

Kid looked surprised and said, "How'd you know."

"Just a wild guess."

We haggled a bit more over what I proclaimed as his exorbitant fee. By that point the whole experience had turned into a good bit of fun. I finally relented and we agreed on another four bits for delivery of my reply.

He gave me back most of the coins I'd initially paid with. Said he wanted paper money. Watched him hotfoot it down the dirt road and thanked my lucky stars I probably wouldn't have to do business with the overly smart little shit as an adult.

4

"... THEY MEAN TO KILL THE BOTH OF US."

Rather than pull Grizz out of the livery for such a short ride, decided I'd walk to the Savage residence. Pleasant stroll cleared my head and lifted sagging spirits. Ever since the dustup in Salt Valley's main thorough-fare, I'd been thinking as how there's just nothing like getting shot in the head to get your undivided attention. Such God-sent events do have the power to set a man to puzzling over his own mortality.

By the time I arrived in front of Mrs. Savage's neatly kept, whitewashed cottage, I felt better than I had in more than a week.

Pushed open the gate on the freshly painted picket fence, crossed the only patch of lush, green grass I'd seen around any of the town's residences, removed my hat, and tapped on the front door. Barely had time to take note of the carefully tended beds of multicolored wildflowers that encircled the entire home.

Dianna Savage answered my knock immediately. Her appearance gave me the distinct impression that the lady had anticipated the visit and spied my approach through one of her curtained front windows.

My God, but the woman's beauty was dazzling for a rough-and-tumble lawdog like me. Stood in the splendid lady's doorway and got right flustered. Stared at my dusty boots and, for several seconds, searched for, but couldn't find, the proper words.

Looking back on that singular event from the vast reaches of time, I know now Dianna had most likely spent the entire afternoon molding herself into an image designed to specifically bring poor defenseless men, like me, to their physical and emotional knees. Suffice it to say, her efforts had exactly the expected effect on one highly impressed, and grateful, Texas Ranger.

Regal, in a dove-gray high-necked dress that probably cost as much as my saddle and emphasized her tiny waist, the lady's simple, unvarnished beauty sucked the breath right out of me. Caught myself staring like a loon at her provocative lips, and almost stumbled backward when a passing breeze tickled my nose with a brand of perfume that made the hair on the back of my neck stand up.

On my third stumbling attempt to speak, she brought a silk kerchief out, dabbed at those inviting lips, then said, "Would you care to come inside, Mr. Dodge?"

Must have looked like a big-eyed colt, and sounded like a half-brained man lookin' to find a corner in a round room when I managed to blurt out, "Why, yes. Indeed I would, Mrs. Savage."

She motioned me into a small, wallpapered parlor located to the left of the front entrance. Decorated with expensive store-bought furniture and heavy wine-colored drapes, the comfortable, homey room was dominated by a rustic stone fireplace that almost covered one whole wall.

She motioned me toward a chair and said, "Please take the brocaded one, Mr. Dodge. It is, by far, the most comfortable seat in the house. Prior to his untimely departure, my husband favored that chair. Loved to bounce William on his knee while sitting in it."

Astonishing woman gracefully slid onto a settee near a delicate-legged end table loaded down with coffee, cups, and cakes. In pretty short order I sported an uncomfortable lap covered by an embroidered cloth napkin, a china cup smaller than a thimble, and at least one of everything she had to offer. Spent the rest of my time in that parlor deathly afraid I'd break something before I could make my escape.

For some minutes we exchanged meaningless pleasantries; then, I noticed that her son was not in evidence. Indirectly approached the subject and said, "And how is young William, Mrs. Savage?"

She shook her head and dabbed at the corner of one eye with her lace hankie. "Well, Mr. Dodge, as well as can be expected, I suppose. William sleeps inordinately of late and is napping at this very moment. I fear the child still evidences a degree of lingering nervousness and apprehension as a result of our recently shared experience."

"My memory of him is of a handsome, bright, and bold youngster. Is there anything I might do to help, Mrs. Savage?"

"Most five-year-old boys eventually recover from just about any trauma, sir. I feel certain my son is no exception." She paused and dropped her gaze, for a second, before continuing. "You know, I thought I had chosen a town so far removed from the vagaries of Texas lawlessness and violence that my son would be completely safe. I fear my judgment may well have failed me in this instance."

She had subtly offered me an entrance into a more personal area of her life with such comments, so I opened the door a bit wider. "Marshal Oakley tells me you came to Salt Valley after your husband died in a tragic fall."

For the first time she offered a slight smile. "The local gossips appear to have been at work again. I fear they often labor much too hard at spreading groundless tales as the truth. No, Mr. Dodge, my husband did not die in a fall. He was murdered by business associates in Shelbyville — a town located in that area of Texas sometimes referred to as the Redlands."

Shook my head in disbelief. "That news is most distressing to hear. Please accept my sympathies for an unacceptable loss."

"Evil men sought to lay their bloody hands on a small fortune he'd acquired through land speculation. But shortly before his death that thoughtful man converted his vast holdings into cash, placed the money in a secret bank account, and informed me how to acquire the funds should anything wayward occur." She fingered a miniature timepiece held to her bodice by a slip of lace. "Looking back on the event, I am almost certain he had a premonition of his brutal passing. Today I am a wealthy woman as a result of his foresight, Mr. Dodge. Perhaps the wealthiest woman in this part of the state."

"And one helluva a shot, I might add." Realized my social blunder immediately. "Forgive my lapse into questionable language, ma'am. I fear my crudity results from rough-and-ready company most of the time."

Pleased me no end when she held the handkerchief over her mouth and cut loose with lusty, robust laughter. "Ah, yes. Well, sir, even my father's extensive investments in Mrs. Cranston's New Orleans Finishing School for Accomplished Young Women did little to erase a rambunctious childhood on the Texas frontier. I was raised in the company of six astonishingly profane brothers. Your 'lapse,' as you call it, is of no consequence."

With that candid confession, she stood and waved me into her dining room and, perhaps, the best home-cooked meal I'd consumed since leaving the shelter of my mother's tender care. When the coffee finally came, and she'd settled back into her chair, I deemed it the best time to broach the topic that actually brought me to her that evening.

Sat my delicate cup in its matching saucer

and said, "Mrs. Savage, I fear we are compelled to discuss a most serious subject before I take my leave from you tonight. I must bring to your attention a matter that could bear heavily upon you and your son's well-being."

Could detect no surprise in her voice, or appearance, at my ominous-sounding declaration. "While I had hoped this visit would remain purely social, and admit to looking forward to seeing you again, sir, I feared that such was the case. I take it you have some news relating to the recent death of the thief Reuben Coffin — by my hand."

Put the cup and saucer aside and leaned toward her in as intimate a gesture as proper deportment would allow. "Marshal Oakley and I have developed what we feel is reliable information that leads us to believe a price has been put on our lives and evil men are on their way to Salt Valley to collect. According to the best information I've been able to develop, those selfsame men mean to kill the both of us."

"And how would you suggest I proceed, Mr. Dodge?"

"As we haven't much time to decide on a course of action, it would be my recommendation that we leave this place as quickly as possible. Seek refuge in Fort Worth. I sincerely doubt even the most determined of killers would follow us into Company B's Ranger camp. Even those bold enough to admit their connection to a man of Nate Coffin's infamous reputation."

Her hand shook as she put her own cup aside. She stood, then strode majestically to one of the windows that faced Salt Valley's central thoroughfare, pulled the curtain aside with one finger, and gazed into a night bathed in gold-tinted moonlight.

"While I must admit to a degree of fear, Mr. Dodge, it is not for my own life, but my son's. William, you see, is my life."

"Please believe that I understand those sentiments completely, ma'am."

"You, and everyone in town, are now privy to my skill with firearms. I can outshoot with rifle or pistol just about any man I've ever met, and have no qualms about exercising my God-given ability if forced to do so."

"An admirable trait, ma'am, but not one I'm sure will help you in this particular instance."

She turned and hit me with an icy stare. "I find your concern for my safety most comforting, Mr. Dodge, but I'll not be rooted out of my home again. William and I came here on a wave of personal tragedy. We aim to stay in Salt Valley no matter what comes our way. Do you understand my feelings on this matter, sir?"

Moved to the lady's side. Touched her forearm and detected no resistance. In fact, she moved ever so slightly my direction. Her shoulder brushed against my chest.

"Marshal Oakley and I are sworn to your protection, both personally and professionally, Mrs. Savage. We'll do whatever is necessary in service of those oaths. But please be advised, Nate Coffin has placed a sizable bounty on both our heads. In his twisted, murderous mind we are responsible for his brother's poor choices in life. The man means to have us dead, and killers are likely on their way as we now speak."

The weight and smell of her became more powerful as she leaned closer and almost whispered, "Let them come, Mr. Dodge. Desperate men might be surprised by a woman determined to protect her son's life, as well as her own, assisted by a valiant Texas Ranger and a stalwart town marshal."

Thought dawned on me, at that exact moment, as how there was simply no more to be said on the subject. Realized she would likely not yield, no matter how keen my reasoning. Besides, my growing infatuation with that stunningly beautiful female simply would not allow me to force the issue.

Took her hand in mine, raised it toward my lips, kissed the back, then said, "Your obedient servant, Mrs. Savage."

She placed her free hand on my arm, then fiddled with a button on my vest. Behind flushed cheeks, she brought her mouth so near my ear I could feel the moist warmth of scented breath. "Please don't think me too bold, sir. But I must admit you are the first man to inspire an almost forgotten feeling of passionate confusion in my blood." Then she quickly moved half a step back, and barely breathed, "Your most ardent admirer, Mr. Dodge."

Surprise doesn't come anywhere near a description of my feelings at that instant. Backed away in delighted bewilderment, mumbled my thanks for the meal, and hastily retreated for the door.

As I stepped onto her small but immaculate porch, she reached out, lightly touched my elbow, and said, "Do come back at your own convenience, Mr. Dodge."

Kissed her hand again and hurried to the gate, but stopped before I reached the street, turned, and said, "I would stay on a bit longer, but fear I cannot trust my judgment as to proper conduct at the moment, Mrs. Savage." Shoved my hat on my head, and damn near ran all the way back to my hotel room.

Spent a sleepless night of constantly raking through every word she had spoken to me, every blissful movement, each and every possibly suggestive gesture. Next morning as I took breakfast with Caleb in my favorite spot on the veranda, explained Dianna's feelings about our combined desires for her safety.

Old marshal didn't mince words. Poked a crisp piece of bacon into his mouth and, through grinding bites, grumbled, "You realize, of course, Coffin's henchmen will come and kill us all, including the child."

Felt convinced of the rightness of my thoughts on the matter. Said, "Oh, I think we'll be reasonably safe, so long as we pay attention and don't do anything stupid."

"Could use a little more experienced help around here, Lucius. My two deputies aren't much more than resident loafers who took the only jobs they could get. Both of 'em are the closest things to bar squeezin's you could dredge up around these parts."

"I'll wire Boz this morning, Caleb. Tell him to get back as fast as good horses can run. He should have delivered Buster into the clutches of the Tarrant County sheriff by now. Man loves a fight. He'll hurry back this way as quickly as possible. Once Tatum arrives, we'll take turns talking with Dianna until we change her mind."

Oakley stroked his chin sagely and said, "Most likely all it'll take to modify Mrs. Savage's rigid attitude is for something ugly and wayward to occur. We can always hope for the best, but as my ole granpappy used to say, 'Hopin' ain't never gonna make it so.'"

Little could I have known that something ugly, wayward, armed to the teeth, and hungry for blood had recently crossed the San Saba River, and would soon fall on all of us like prairie thunder. Bloody death was coming to Salt Valley.

5

"AMAZING WHAT TWO GALLONS OF COAL OIL CAN DO."

Cannot bring to mind a single circumstance worse than being awakened from a sound sleep by the distant, distinct, and persistent sound of gunfire — lots of gunfire. If you ply the lawdog's trade for any time at all, such events usually slap you with the unavoidable foggy-minded conclusion that someone has probably died as a result of a rudely applied dose of hot lead. Snapped to consciousness in my hotel room and instinctively knew that the remote blasting I heard came from a spot out past Salt Valley's sawmill — Dianna Savage's house.

Sat bolt upright and thumped onto the floor in my sock feet. Got somewhat dressed. Grabbed my pistol belt, rifle, and boots on the way out the door. Stumbled into the hotel lobby still bootless. Burst through the door, dropped to the edge of the boardwalk, and hastily pulled the boots on.

Hit the street just in time for Marshal Oakley to thunder up on a long-legged bay mare. He led an already saddled hay burner for me. Disheveled and flushed, the visibly concerned lawman appeared to have been aroused in the exact same fashion as I had.

Couldn't help but notice the pained expression on his weather-beaten face. "Gotta hurry, Lucius. Sounds like someone's trying to level the Savage place."

Leapt aboard a strange animal and kicked north. Hadn't even got past the town's limits when the shooting abruptly stopped. About a minute later, we roared up to what was left of Dianna's picket fence. The horse was still running when I jumped off, hit the ground like a rabid, slobbering wolf, and broke through her bullet-riddled front door, fully ready to kill anything out of place.

Flew past the shattered entrance and almost stepped on her. Spattered and smeared with splotches of fresh blood from toe to crown, she kneeled on the floor amidst piles of broken glass, splintered shards of wood, and a growing pool of slick gore. Trembling arms encircled the shattered body of young William. Child had all the appearance of a twisted, colorless doll drenched in dark, sticky liquid.

Of a sudden, a sound unlike any I'd ever

heard in my entire life rose from somewhere deep inside the distraught mother's heaving chest and clawed its way past her constricted throat. Something between a screech and an agonized moan, the noise she made caused rippling gooseflesh all over my back, and the hairs rose up on my arms and neck. Closest thing I could compare it to would be the call of the most lonesome mountain lion in west Texas.

"They've killed my baby," she shrieked, and rocked back and forth on bloody knees as she clutched at the dead child. "Oh, my dear God, they've killed my baby." She couldn't stop saying it. Over and over, the same thing. "They've killed my beautiful baby. Sweet forgiving Jesus, they've killed my only child. Oh, my God in Heaven."

Knelt beside the stricken girl and tried to offer some comfort, but in my experience, there is no consolation for such intense agony. She must have wept gallons before Caleb and I finally separated her from the lifeless body of her poor, dead son. As her last fingertip slipped from his cold, limp hand, she moaned piteously and collapsed in a heap at my feet.

We wrapped William's tiny corpse in a hand-knitted comforter and delivered it into the care of a Mr. Arliss Heavner, who built caskets in Salt Valley and conducted funerals. By then, some of the town ladies had arrived. They swooped in and formed a sweet-smelling knot of weeping sympathy around the devastated Dianna. Shooed all us menfolk outside and away from an agony so pervasive it affected even the hardest of those who appeared on the scene to offer their help and concern.

Caleb and I stood in Dianna's once-beautiful, now ravaged front yard and rolled ourselves a smoke. He took his first lungful, blew it heavenward, then muttered, "Front of this place looks like twenty men spent an hour firing into it."

"Couldn't have been more'n two or three of 'em," I said, "according to the tracks they left behind. Maybe four. Headed off to the south and west. Arrogant scum didn't even bother to make an effort to cover their trail. Guess they were in too big a hurry. Bastards did one helluva job. Can't even imagine how Mrs. Savage survived a fusillade of such deadly intensity and came out of it pretty much unscathed."

Old marshal lowered his head. "She didn't come out unscathed. Not by a damn sight." He took another puff from his smoke. "You know, Lucius, given the trail they left, if we head out now, could probably catch up with 'em 'fore the end of the day. Kill 'em all or, better yet, have 'em swingin' from a tree limb by this time tomorrow." He hard-eyed me and waited.

Shook my head and said, "No. While I wholeheartedly agree with the sentiment, probably best we stay here till young William is buried. Mrs. Savage will need as much support as can be provided from everyone she knows."

"Longer we wait, the more difficult it'll be to catch 'em. You know that as well as I do."

"Well, with any luck at all, Boz should have my wire in hand by now. He'll be on his way back pretty damned quick. Man has the uncanny ability to track a water spider across a muddy puddle. Don't fret. Boz and I'll find this pack of killers no matter where they run. They're nothin' but dead men ridin' horses."

To tell the absolute truth, I firmly believed every word of what I said to Caleb that unfortunate morning. But as often occurs, fate has other directions in mind for us, and bides its time for the right moment to show a man what the future has in store. For me, it happened the following afternoon at a tree-shaded graveyard that no longer exists on the far western edge of Salt Valley, Texas.

Back in those terrible times you had to

get the dead into the ground as quickly as possible. No letting the dearly departed sit around for a week at a stretch while the family gathered from the four points of the compass. Grief often had to wait till a more convenient day and hour. Not really much time for mourning your losses. Had to put folks in the ground and get on with your life.

Salt Valley didn't have access to anything like a sufficient supply of ice. As a consequence, there existed no way to preserve young William's tiny, pitiful corpse at that juncture. So, Dianna and most of the town's suffering citizens gathered in the Little Angels section of the Pecan Grove Cemetery for her son's interment, just before dusk the day after his brutal murder.

My God, but the sunset that sad afternoon can only be described as nothing short of glorious. Streaks of red, orange, and soft purple darted across all of heaven, from a molten sun that appeared to boil the earth as it slid out of view on the far side of the world.

A number of those who attended said, a few minutes before dark in the soft shadows of approaching twilight, it appeared to them as though God had provided that stunning evening as a special dispensation for having taken an unblemished soul before its time. Dianna asked that I escort her to the graveside. Her innocent child's numerous wounds had forced a closed coffin.

Grieving girl leaned heavily on my arm. Wept pitifully as the sad-eyed Mr. Heavner read several short passages from the Bible, then led the assembled group in a prayer. Brief, heartrending service ended with a mournful rendition of the old hymn "Yes, We'll Gather at the River." Tears flowed from all but the hardest of hearts.

First shovel of clods had barely thumped against the lid on his diminutive coffin when William's red-eyed mother pulled me away from the moist smell of fresh-turned earth. We stopped beside her carriage, parked near the cemetery's wildflower-embellished entrance. She gazed off in the direction of a barely visible fingernail of remaining sunlight. God's glorious orb had blended into the earth's distant crest and left little more than a sliver of its silent passing.

"We'll start out after the men who did this tomorrow morning," she said, without taking her eyes away from the vanishing light.

"What on earth are you thinking, Dianna? You're not going anywhere."

She pulled me around so our faces were only inches apart. Even in the advancing twilight I could detect a new, aggressive, and more hardened look at the corners of her remarkable eyes.

"I mean to begin the hunt at break of day tomorrow, Lucius. Be at my house loaded for bear and ready to ride. I'll be waiting. We're going after the men who killed my son, before they get too far away to catch."

"You don't know what you're saying. Whoever they are, we know one thing about them for certain. They're cold-eyed killers who have absolutely no qualms about the slaughter of women and children. Given that knowledge, even approaching such men could be dangerous in the extreme. No place for a woman."

A barely perceptible smile cut across her face like a wound created by an ax. "I don't intend to approach anyone, Lucius. My aim is to kill them before they even realize that death is standing by their worthless sides. And once I've done with them, Nate Coffin is next. The man won't live out the next month, if I have anything to say about it."

"All that might be a good bit harder to accomplish than you think. We should wait for Boz Tatum's return. I've sent an urgent telegraph to Fort Worth. He should be here within a week's time."

"No. We cannot, must not, tarry — even

for a single wasted minute. You've already witnessed my ability with a pistol. Fought the Comanche with my father, but have little skill as a tracker. You'll find the men who murdered my son, and, together, we'll send all of them to Satan. I expect to see every last one of those skunks dead for what they did to William, and for their manifest other sins I'm certain we know nothing of." Then, as if an afterthought, she added, "That includes the scurrilous bastard Nate Coffin for sending them."

"Mighty strong talk."

"Nothing like strong talk, Lucius. It's a sworn promise. I swear before the God who watched over this uncalled-for funeral today that, even if you don't show up, I'll go after them myself."

"What about Caleb? He'll want to come along too."

She squeezed my arm. "Don't tell Caleb. He'll just slow us down."

Probably would have done what she wanted anyway. But when that sad, beautiful girl pressed her body against mine and kissed me so gently that I barely felt the brush of her full, voluptuous lips, whatever resistance I might have harbored crumbled like heat-withered flowers on her son's newly dug grave.

She squeezed my hand and said, "You will be there tomorrow, won't you?" Came out more like a statement than a question.

"I owe you a sacred debt that can never be repaid, Dianna. Not sure what my life is worth. But chasing down William's killers, and perhaps ridding the world of Nate Coffin, should be a good beginning on the obligation. So, yes, I'll be there. And promise, by whatever means necessary, to help you kill 'em all."

She turned for the carriage. I helped her climb aboard, and placed the reins in hands that still trembled. "Be waiting for you at sunup," she said. And with the snap of her buggy whip, she left me standing in a cloud of swirling Texas dust outside the sadly forlorn Pecan Grove graveyard. Shook my head and wondered if either of us would live through the following week.

Spent the rest of that evening in preparation for the hunt. Bought a mule at the only livery in town. Provisioned it with enough food and ammunition for an extended chase. Figured the killers wouldn't be foolish enough to spend much time in a town and that we'd spend most of our time living on the ground.

Cleaned, loaded, and checked all my weapons. It's never a good idea to brace dangerous men with a rifle, pistol, or shotgun you've mistakenly forgotten to charge for a fight or to test for possible mechanical failure. Many a man has died as a result of such feebleminded carelessness.

'Course, you can never really know exactly what desperate killers on the run will do. Some want to get away from the scene of their gruesome activities as quickly as possible. Such men won't stop legging it until they feel safe. Others will hit the first dram shop available, drink themselves into near oblivion over the guilt they feel for their hideous criminality. Still others will drink, raise almighty hell, and brag to anyone who'll listen about the brutality of their most recent repugnant offense. Worst of all, some murderers gleefully run directly to their next atrocity.

True to her word, Dianna sat on the porch of her devastated house the next morning. She had one of the finest-looking buckskin mares I've ever seen saddled, ready, and tied to the hitch rail out by the road. Animal stamped one front foot and snorted when I rode up. Appeared more than anxious to get on the trail. Stepped down from Grizz and started toward the porch. Sharp, oily smell wafted up my nose on a slight, hot breeze.

Guess I hadn't gone two steps in the grieving woman's direction when she stood, scratched a lucifer to life, and pitched it into the front door. Dressed like a man in pants, boots, a palm-leaf sombrero, and sporting a fine bone-gripped Colt's pistol strapped high on her waist, she turned, closed the door, and jumped off the porch. The house exploded in a ferocious ball of scorching fire behind her. Rocked on its foundation. Sparkling shards of shattered glass filled the air on waves of angry flame.

Gal strode past me and never looked back. Bent over, snatched a gallon-sized metal can off the ground, and headed for the mule.

"Amazing what two gallons of coal oil can do," she said over her shoulder as she tied the can to the mule's load with our other supplies.

Stood in what was left of her once-well-kept yard and watched as the fast-moving conflagration spread to a wood-shingled roof, consumed the porch, and hungrily licked at the outside walls through blackened, shattered windows.

Couldn't do anything 'cept shake my head in amazement. Over the years, I've come to realize that it does absolutely no good whatever to question why women do the things they do. As men, our best course of action is to simply stand back in amazement, and wait until they get ready to explain their actions. Gave up trying to figure it out and followed her to the horses. By the time I could get myself mounted, she'd already made it across the road and had pointed the buckskin along the wide, clear trail left by her son's killers.

Before good dark we crossed the San Saba, and almost made it to the Llano. Set up our first camp under an ancient live oak on a rolling hillside. A rock-filled, clear-running creek wandered south toward the river less than five miles away.

Determined pretty quick I might have to try and get Dianna to slow down a bit. Girl's fired-up determination and single-minded desire for revenge had the potential for playing havoc on our animals. And if we overtook the killers at the wrong time, it could prove fatal for the both of us.

Picketed the horses, then got a fire going. Dianna volunteered to take care of the meals. That suited me right down to the ground. Never professed any real talent at a cook fire. I could produce a fair pot of coffee in a pinch. Boz forced me into permanently taking on that particular chore when we hit the trail together.

Couldn't tell exactly how he accomplished

it, but my Ranger compadre did something to coffee grounds that defied imagination or understanding. Never tasted such uncommon bilge in my entire life. Fascinating part of the whole deal was that Boz loved the foul-tasting stuff. He derisively referred to my brew as "weak-assed belly wash," and said it didn't have any more taste than mildly muddy water — but he never turned down a single cup.

With the scent of wild bluebonnets drifting on an evening breeze that barely stirred the air, we finished our meal and stowed the gear. Stretched my tired, aching body out on my blanket. Dianna dropped into her bed like a felled tree. Thought she went right to sleep.

Surprised me some when, as if talking to the sky, she said, "Do you think we can catch up with them before they make it back to Uvalde?"

"Well, don't appear as though they're in any hurry. Probably figure so much lead got poured into your house, it killed everyone they wanted dead. Way we've been ridin', like early don't last long enough, just might catch up to 'em any time. Specially if they stop, or get careless."

"Maybe I'll pray for *careless* tonight."

"Gotta be more cautious ourselves from

now on, Dianna. Save our mounts. Might have to run 'em hard if these boys spot us."

She rolled onto her side and faced me across our dying fire. "Whatever may come tomorrow, or whenever we catch up with them, I want at least one of those murdering skunks alive."

"Thought you wanted to kill 'em all."

She closed tired eyes and snuggled deeper into her blanket. "Oh, he won't live long after I've had a chance to talk to him. Bet he'll even beg me to end it all before I've finished."

"Sounds like you think you're up to torture if necessary."

Barely heard it, but pretty sure she said, "You'd be surprised what I'm up to, or capable of, Ranger Dodge. Completely and totally amazed."

God Almighty, but Dianna's bald-faced threat sounded powerful ominous. Never would have figured such venom from the woman, but given what had been brutally taken from her, couldn't blame the angry gal one little bit. Thought on the whole doo-dah for some time that night. Eventually came to the inescapable conclusion that had I found myself in the beautiful widow Savage's position, eating bees and biting the horns off the Devil in his own parlor would have only been the beginning of my bloody retribution. 'Fore I fell asleep, said a silent prayer that Boz would catch up right quick. Always best to have another gun on such a raid. Good God, but I didn't want to make a mistake and get me and Dianna killed.

6

"YOU BEEN SEEIN' SPIRITS, MRS. SAVAGE?"

Mid-morning of the following day, we topped a rock-strewn, scrubby, mesquite-covered hill that overlooked Indian Creek. Some miles farther to the south, the free-flowing stream emptied into the Llano. Three hundred yards below our vantage point, an unfinished cabin constructed of logs and rough-cut planks almost glowed in the warmth of a rising sun.

Rail corral attached to the west end of the incomplete house showed empty. Lean-to shed on the east side was near hidden under the sheltering shade of a sixty-foot-tall cottonwood shaped like a gigantic umbrella. A flock of skinny chickens wandered about in the grassless yard.

The massive tree dropped puffy white balls in such quantities, the entire silent place appeared as though covered by a layer of summertime snow. Hot, gently wafting breezes carried the tree's droppings of the cottony stuff in drifts that piled hand-sized wads against every upright surface available. An unnatural hush, occasionally punctuated by the raspy call of locusts, presented the entire area in an eerie, otherworldly, grayish-white shroud.

Strained to get an informative look through my long glass. "Appears the front door's open, but I can't see anyone movin' about," I said. "Not even any animals, other than the chickens, in evidence. Trail leads right to the front door, though. If the men we're after aren't here, you can wager the family fortune they've been here. Lord help anyone down there who got in their way."

Dianna snatched the glass from my grasp. "Let me see," she said.

After several seconds of scanning the scene for herself, she handed the scope back, removed her dusty hat, and slapped it against an equally encrusted leg. "Be willing to take that bet. Appears the skunks we're chasing have been here and gone already, Lucius. God only knows what the murderous scum left behind."

Pulled and cocked a pistol. Gently urged Grizz down the hill. Over my shoulder, said, "Stay here with the mule while I give the place a good going-over. Shouldn't take long. Wait till I call you in."

Heard no objections from Dianna, and when I glanced back that way, she still sat her buckskin and hadn't moved. Almost made it to the silent hut's front door before I spotted what appeared to be a man's body stretched on the floor inside.

Pulled up, stepped down, and let my reins drop to the ground. Patted Grizz's neck and whispered, "Stand, Grizz, stand." Animal nibbled at my hand and snorted. Knew he wouldn't move, no matter what transpired.

Kept the pistol pointed at the house and, with my free hand, loosened the bindings on my short-barreled shotgun. Pulled the big popper and snapped it open with my left hand. Both barrels were primed. Snapped it shut, and headed for the door. Felt considerable better once I had the big blaster in hand.

Do not to this very day know exactly why, but there's just something spine-chilling about approaching the scene of a freshly discovered and brutal murder. Had been in such a state of belligerence the day I burst into Dianna's house, those feelings had somehow managed to go right over my head at the time. But as I approached the half-built, cotton-covered house on Indian Creek, an uncomfortable feeling of sinister forces, perhaps lurking nearby, came over me in an unsettling wave of apprehension.

Carefully eased my way to the open door. Based on what I could see, the dead feller couldn't have been any more than twenty-five or thirty years old. Obvious to me his killers had surprised hell out of him with a bullet to the eye when he opened the door. Powder burns on one whole cheek of a contorted face led me to believe that whoever fired the fatal shot must have been right on top of him. Looked like they'd shoved the muzzle right into his eye. Jesus, what a bloody mess.

Stepped over the corpse. Did a quick, nerve-rattled inspection of the single twelve-by-twenty-foot room. Littered floor and overturned, broken furniture presented the image of a formerly well-kept home where not a single item now resided in its intended place. Only good thing I could say about the scene was that no other dead folk appeared in evidence.

Noise from behind got my attention. Jumped and brought the shotgun around only to find Dianna standing in the doorway. Girl held her cocked pistol ready for action, and shook her head in disgust.

"Thought I told you to wait up on the hill," I said. "Could've shot you dead, girl.

Shouldn't sneak up on an agitated man like that."

"I did exactly as you told me, but felt I'd waited long enough. Thought came to me that, perhaps, you might need some help. Of course I can now see that you don't. Have you found the woman yet?"

"Woman? What woman is that? What makes you think there's a woman?"

"Better take a good look, Ranger Dodge. Dead or alive, there must be a woman around somewhere."

"How can you tell?"

Sounded a bit frustrated with me when she snapped, "Furnishings, curtains on the windows, broom by the door, place is spotless, except for the overturned furniture and such. Haven't known a man yet who didn't live like a hibernating bear when left to his own devices."

"Now that's a bit harsh, don't you think?"

"Most of you hairy-legged types should take up residence in caves alongside some other of God's beasts. The men we're after came, killed the husband" — she pointed at the stiff with her pistol — "ransacked the house, and took the woman. Either that, or we'll find her body somewhere nearby. Then, they wisely ran like God was after them."

Already had most of Dianna's rendition of the available facts figured out for myself. Pleased me some, though, that she'd come to much the same conclusions. Really quite impressive for a female, once I'd thought it over a bit.

We headed outside and searched every nook and cranny, and under all the rocks within a hundred yards of the spooky place. Couldn't find a single trace of a woman — other than an extra set of tracks mixed in with those we'd followed all the way from Salt Valley. Had intended to leave the dead feller where he fell, but Dianna wouldn't hear of it.

"I will not depart this place and continue our pursuit until that poor unfortunate man is buried. It's the only proper thing to do, Mr. Dodge."

She rummaged around in all the disorder and came up with a family Bible. Flipped through the pages and said, "Appears from this that the dead man's name was Luther Wainwright. Hails from over near Mexia. Took a lady named MaryLou Bookbinder of Nacogdoches as his bride a mere six months past. Absolutely shameful good folk like these should suffer at the hands of the animals we're after. Poor man deserves whatever we can supply in the way of a

Christian burial, however paltry."

Damned if she didn't head outside, locate a shovel, and go to digging the hole her very own self. Well, she'd shamed me as much as necessary. I stripped off my pistol belt and hat, gently took the spade from her, and finished off the rough grave myself.

Not enough time to put poor Mr. Wainwright down as deep as we probably should have. Found a stack of sizable rocks at the end of the house near the corral. Looked as though they'd been intended for use around his unfinished fireplace. Piled most of them on the grave. Figured he wouldn't be building a cozy fire anytime soon. By then, the sun had made it right low in the sky.

"We could stay here for the night," I said, and wiped the grit and sweat from my face on my sleeve.

"No, I'll not tarry where this poor man died. We'll move on a bit farther. There's still a bit of light left."

"You afraid of ghosts by any chance, Dianna?"

Hadn't noticed before, but hot tears rolled down both her cheeks as she turned away from me. "I'm not afraid of them, but prefer not to have any contact with the spirits of those who've passed at this particular place and time."

"Spirits? You been seein' spirits, Mrs. Savage?"

"Unfortunately, yes. That's precisely why I burned my house, Mr. Dodge. I saw William the night after we buried him. He came to the foot of my bed. Swear I felt him touch my foot. He told me that Heaven was a beautiful place. Said everything was all right, and that I must not worry about him. I must admit to being profoundly affected by that vision, Lucius. As a consequence, I'll not stay in the unfortunate Mr. Wainwright's sad home tonight."

Not much of a way to reason with such feelings, so I let it go and pointed us south again. We arrived on the banks of the Llano before hard dark set in. Camped in a sheltered spot, next to the river, surrounded by a stand of beautiful live oaks.

Felt we'd best not light a fire given our possible proximity to the killers we chased. The inconvenience mattered little, as the weather smiled on us, and we had a good moon as well. Made a meal of jerky, cold biscuits, and a jar of home-made muscadine jam I had bought from the general mercantile in Salt Valley.

Dianna leaned across her saddle and watched with some curiosity as I scraped up a final tasty morsel of the preserves with my knife. Surprised me when she said, "My husband had a weakness for sweets. I've come to the belief that most men harbor the same soft spot. Haven't met one yet who didn't exhibit an unbridled appetite for sugar. Those who can't get it any other way resort to the debilitating rigors of liquor."

"Well, now, you know, that could be true. Hadn't thought on it much myself. Some men *are* given to excess drink. Some eat too much, others chase loose women of every shape, size, and disposition. I love sugar in virtually all its forms. Especially partial to jams and jellies slathered on a good biscuit. These sourdough bullets of yours are right tasty, Mrs. Savage. Perhaps the combination reminds me of my mother and a pleasantly countrified childhood on the family ranch near Lampasas."

Must have hit a number of soft spots concerning her murdered spouse. She turned away for a spell, then out of the clear blue said, "We met in New Orleans. Mr. Savage used to herd cattle up from Corpus Christi along the Gulf Coast. Extremely dangerous business then, and now. After a number of years at such hazardous work, he wanted to settle down. Have children. Live to a ripe and satisfied old age. That's why we moved to San Augustine and, less than a year later, to what we'd hoped was the even tamer clime of Shelbyville. Fooled us. Seems bad people do, in fact, inhabit even the most docile-appearing corners of the earth."

"You've described almost every living man's hopes for the future. Suppose we'd all like as much, Dianna. Just that sometimes life has ways of not working out how we wanted — or even halfway expected. Know mine hasn't. Had my druthers, I'd still be working cattle on Pa's ranch over on the Colorado, and he'd be alive and bouncing chubby-cheeked grandkids on his bony knees. But a land-greedy killer named Slayton Bone changed all that."

Even in the semidarkness, I could see her eyes sparkle under the moon's caressing glow. "You've hit upon the single most powerful thing the two of us have in common, Mr. Dodge. Family and loved ones dead at the hands of evil men."

Must admit she surprised me with the depth and power of her feelings. "Please forgive my insensitivity for resurrecting bad memories so close to your recent loss," I said.

"Oh, don't feel obligated to tiptoe around the obvious. Life does go on. Death is the one constant all of us must live with every day. While I grieve over the violent departures of my husband and son, the realization that such events are nothing more than part of God's great plan is also ever with me."

"Nonetheless, I could have been more thoughtful."

"No, you're about as considerate as any man I've met in years, Ranger Dodge." She rolled into her bed, and thus ended the conversation.

We caught up with them killers two days later near a stack of enormous boulders called Enchanted Rock. They had slowed down even more than I expected. Fairly certain at the time that the captive woman had probably caused it.

Bunch couldn't have been any more than a quarter of a mile away when I checked their progress through my long glass. We'd stopped on a low, mesquite-covered hill. Thought for a second I detected part of the reason for our luck.

"Think one of their horses might have gone lame," I mumbled. "Most likely picked up one of these mesquite thorns somehow. Then again, could be they're about to pull up for a spell of takin' turns abusin' Mary-Lou Wainwright."

Dianna shook her head like a tired dog,

then stared at gloved hands. "God Almighty, give me strength. Mr. Dodge, it just doesn't matter one way or the other why we've caught up with the murderous skunks. Any help the Good Lord, or Providence, sees fit to provide is just fine. I'll pray for the unfortunate Mrs. Wainwright's speedy deliverance through any kind of earthly intervention, and supply it myself given the chance."

"Well, the whole crew is a-draggin' pretty good. Looks like they're gonna have to stop right soon. Bet next month's near-to-nothin' Ranger pay they're searchin' for an out-of-the-way ranch so they can break in, eat, misuse the poor lady, and perhaps steal another mount. Hell, they could even be lookin' for another woman, for all we know, right now."

She leaned over, grabbed my sleeve, and said, "Are you absolutely certain these are the men who killed my son, Mr. Dodge?"

Question surprised me a bit. "Well, have to admit as how I didn't see 'em do the infamous deed, but these are the same men we tracked from the house you burned to the ground, and the scene of Luther Wain-wright's brutal murder. There's four of 'em — one obviously a woman. Would be will-ing to bet everything I've got they're the men we want. Never been wrong about anything like this before, Mrs. Savage."

She slid her model '73 Winchester out and levered a shell into the chamber. "Can we run 'em to ground before it gets dark?"

Thought on that one a spell before I volunteered, "We'll let 'em get to the other side of that rise they're on. Then we'll really burn saddle leather. Shouldn't be able to see or hear us coming. Be on their backs so fast, they'll never know what hit 'em." She nodded her approval.

We sat our horses and waited for the killing to start.

7

"BULLET NEARLY TOOK HIS HEAD OFF."

Played our deadly hand exactly the way I described it for Dianna. Soon as our murderous quarry vanished from sight, we put the spurs to our animals and headed out like a pair of six-legged bobcats. That gal rode a horse with all the abandon of a painted Comanche on a kill-all-the-white-devils raiding party. She stayed ahead of me the entire way.

Finally dropped the reins on the mule and set my chaps to flapping. Hit the crest of the rise a few lengths behind Dianna, and damn near rode over those surprised boys. They'd pulled up in a flat, grassy, open area in the trail to cuss and confer with the man whose horse limped.

Killers' thunderstruck captive sat on a rock nearby. Couldn't attest, then or now, as to whether she saw or heard one thing that happened when we burst in on the trail-side confab. Only know the much-abused lady never moved a muscle, nor appeared to blink an unseeing eye.

Dianna got to them boys first. Kicked her cayuse into a dead run and darted right through the middle of their hastily called prayer meeting. Before any of the faithful could fill their blood-soaked hands, she stood in her stirrups and shot two of them. Had turned and headed for the third man when he threw up his hands, fell on terrified knees, and went to begging for mercy.

Astounded is the only word powerful enough to describe how I felt at that moment. Always believed hitting anything from horseback at a dead run rated as a damned good trick, but that angry black-haired gal had just managed the feat twice in a matter of seconds. Grieving lady was a helluva lot more of an Indian fighter than I would ever have been inclined to believe. One thing I know for damned certain. Just ain't nothing like watching an accomplished practitioner of the man-killing trade work, and, by God, Dianna Savage was beyond good at the craft. Couldn't do anything but shake my head in stunned amazement.

Reined Grizz to a jumping stop, and hopped down. Disarmed both them ole boys she'd plugged. Wild-eyed gal's blood was still high and running hot. She fogged up from the other direction and jumped off her snorting animal like a south Texas brush popper about to brand a sharp-hoofed, uncooperative calf.

Gal continued to surprise me with her capability for brutality. She stomped over to the feller who'd recently got religion, and whacked him a good 'un across his yammering noggin with her rifle barrel. Sounded like someone dropped a basket full of eggs. Opened up a gash six inches long right in the middle of his scalp. Poor son of a gun yelped, rolled onto his side, and flopped like a beached fish.

Then, as God is my witness, she turned, threw a hate-filled glance at the men she'd just put life-stealing holes in, and snarled, "Are both those child-killing sons of Satan finished?"

Pointed at one of the men she'd managed to hit and said, "Well, this 'un here's bought a hole in the ground for good and certain. You got him in the neck. Shot through and through. Bullet nearly took his head off. Gonna bleed out right where he hit the ground."

Never missed a beat when she snapped, "Good."

"But your aim must have failed a mite on this other one. Punched a hole in him right under the heart — that is, if he's got one. He's still twitchin' some. Figure he'll be gone soon, though. Then again, you never know. Seen men shot as bad or worse who survived and lived on."

Think she said, "Good," again, but have to admit I didn't exactly hear her final assessment of the matter. Vengeance-minded girl's bloodthirsty attention had swung back to the feller with the split scalp. He sat up, rubbed at the spot where Dianna had bounced her weapon off his head, found blood, and went to grousing about getting whacked with a rifle barrel. Watched as she strode to his side and prodded him up with the same instrument she'd used on his newly damaged and freely bleeding brain box.

"Move your more than sorry self over there with your worthless friends," she ordered, and jabbed him hard in the ribs.

He yelped and struggled almost erect on wobbly legs. Started hobbling my direction. Guess the poor, stupid goober didn't move fast enough to suit her. She kicked his narrow behind so hard, I thought her boot would come out his mouth. He whooped like a surprised dog and fell to his knees again. Went to hollerin' about how he'd never seen any "decent" lady act in such a brutal, inhuman, and unchristian manner.

My God, but that was the wrong thing to say to a woman on a mission like Dianna. All I could do was stand back in amazement. My best plan of action seemed to be to stay out of her hair. Let the situation play out however it would.

So red-faced I thought her head might explode, she clomped right up to him, leaned to within inches of his face, and snapped, "You killed my beautiful baby, you sorry cur. His name was William Tyler Savage, after his father. Then, more recently, as you attempted to escape that killing, you murdered a poor innocent man who never did you any harm. And from all visible evidence, have reduced his innocent wife to witless insensibility. In a few minutes I will arrange for you to shake hands with Satan. Before you go, though, you're gonna tell us everything you ever knew about who sent you to Salt Valley to perform cowardly murder on a woman and small child."

As though struck by lightning, the good-for-nothing skunk seemed to finally grasp an inkling of the actual depth of his predicament. "God Almighty," he squeaked, "you're the woman what kilt Reuben Coffin?"

Dianna's voice sounded like a knife tip dragged across flint. "Thought me dead, I suspect. Figured you'd sent me to Jesus, just like that poor woman's husband. Well, you were wrong, dead wrong, you gutless wretch. I'll give you enough time to make your peace with God; then I'm inclined to kill you deader than Davy Crockett."

In a pose of trembling supplication, our only living killer slobbered, "Swear 'fore all the saints in God's blue heaven, lady, I never fired a single shot at your house. It were mostly them boys you done kilt — Fez and Jethro Parker yonder. Both of 'em heartless bastards, if'n there ever lived men you could call such." He pointed a shaking finger at his shot-to-hell friends. "That 'un with the hole in his neck was Fez. Think your partner done allowed as how Jethro might still be living."

Dianna's voice went colder than a Montana well rope in January. "What's your name?"

Her question caught him by surprise. Our talkative captive appeared to feel he'd dodged a death-dealing bullet. Think for a spell he actually believed he'd spotted a softening, or weakness, in his female tormentor.

Right proud, he smiled, and through bloody teeth bragged, "Name's Burl Tiner, but everyone calls me Smoky, ma'am. You can call me Smoky, if'n you'd like."

"Well, Smoky," she growled, "I want you to watch what I'm about to do — very carefully."

Gal legged it over to Jethro Parker's still-convulsing body, levered a shell into her rifle, and shot him right between the eyes. Busted that ole boy's skull all to pieces. Bone, blood, pieces of scalp, and hair sprayed in every direction.

Don't know who was most surprised, me or Smoky Tiner. Been my experience that it's always one thing to say you'll do a thing, another to actually do it. She'd said she would kill them all. Way she dispatched Jethro Parker made a born-again believer out of me. Scared the literal hell out of Smoky. Man covered his face and cried like a baby.

"Oh, Jesus. Save me, Jesus. Come help me, Jesus," Tiner squealed. "Good God Almighty. I ain't done nothin', lady. Swear to you on my dear sainted mother's grave. Them boys done all the shootin'. I jist held their horses."

Slowed him down some when he felt the muzzle of her rifle against his ear. "Oh, God. Oh, God. Oh, God. Please don't shoot me, missez. Ask me anything. I'll tell you whatever you want to know. Do anything.

Anything at all. Just please don't shoot."

Sounded like an agitated mother wolf when she snarled, "Who sent you to my home with murder in your black heart?"

"Nate Coffin, ma'am. He done it. Paid us money, he did. Hundred dollars each. Said he'd give us another five hundred when we got back and he knew for sure you wuz dead as a lightnin'-struck tree."

"You're certain of that?" I asked. Tiner turned from Dianna and looked at me like I'd lost my mind. "Coffin sent you boys himself?" I went on.

"Hell, yes. Think I'm stupid or somethin'? Known the man for five years. It were Coffin sure as big black bears piss in the woods. Pardon me, ma'am. Let my mouth get ahead of my thinker box. Meant no offense."

Dianna jabbed the nervous killer with her rifle again. "How do you know Nate Coffin?"

Tiner flinched like she was killing him. "We 'uz workin' for the man over in Uvalde. Stole livestock for 'im. Ole Nate has cattle-stealin' camps like our'n all over south Texas. He come up over a week ago from his big ranch house, down near Carrizo Springs, to check on our operation. He'd got news that day as how you'd done went and kilt his little brother Reuben. Man went crazy wild. Said he'd pay a handsome price to any of us willing to rid the world of your shadow."

"Have any idea where Coffin is now?" I asked.

"Far as I'd know, he's probably back at the ranch. Don't get far away from that 'ere place, 'less he has to."

"Don't lie this late in the game," Dianna snapped. "You don't want to stand before your Maker with a falsehood on your lips."

"Swear 'fore Jesus, lady. I ain't a-lyin'."

Dianna raised her Winchester and aimed at Tiner's head. Forced me to step in and touch her on the shoulder. "Why don't you see to Mrs. Wainwright. Let me talk with Smoky some more. You've got plenty of time to kill him, and he might be able to provide us with more in the way of needed information."

As if recovering from a trance, she shook her head, then lowered the weapon. Turned toward the vacant-eyed woman perched on the rock. Cold as ice, Dianna said, "All right, Ranger Dodge. You talk with this skunk all you want. But if I have anything to do with his highly questionable future, the belly-slinking slug won't see tomorrow's sun come up."

She turned, headed over to MaryLou Wainwright, and placed a sympathetic hand on the mute woman's shoulder. Could barely hear Dianna as she tried to offer words of comfort to someone who looked as if she might well be beyond such efforts.

Tiner got my attention when he pulled at my sleeve like a chastised child and whined, "You ain't a-gonna let her kill me, are you, Ranger?"

Never got a chance to answer his question. Dianna huffed back over and snapped, "We've got to get her to a doctor soon as possible. What these bastards must have done to this unfortunate woman goes beyond anything I could have conjured up in a nightmare."

"Willow Junction is about fifteen miles away. Them folks have a fine sawbones in residence. Leastways had one last time I passed through. Also have a city marshal and jail. We can get Mrs. Wainwright cared for, deposit Tiner in the calaboose, and put up for the night in the Cattleman's Hotel. Sleep in a real bed. How's that sound?"

She side-glanced at Tiner, and for a second or so, appeared torn between my suggestion and making good on her threat to finish him off. After about ten seconds of puzzlement, she said, "Fine with me. Let's get moving. Not sure how long this lady can last if we don't see to her needs. Appears her mind might have snapped."

"We gonna bury these dead fellers?" Felt I already knew the answer, but thought the question needed to be asked.

She threw a calloused and fleeting glimpse at the corpses. Said, "They can rot where they fell. I'm far more troubled about Mrs. Wainwright's condition right now." She pointed at Tiner with her rifle again. "Put that yellowbelly on a horse before I change my mind and kill him right here."

Smoky almost fell all over himself in an effort to thank me for saving his sorry neck. "Sweet Jesus, Ranger, thought I wuz a goner for sure and certain. Cain't thank you enough."

"Don't be thanking me before the fact."

"What you mean by that?" he said as he climbed on his horse.

"Well, it's just that she's not finished with you yet, ole son. Real good chance you might not make Willow Junction if'n that angry, heartbroken female takes a notion to snuff your lamp 'fore we get there."

He shot a sneaky peek at Dianna as she helped Mrs. Wainwright get mounted. "You're kiddin', aren't you?"

Climbed on Grizz. "Nope. Not kiddin' in

the least. Best keep your mouth shut and your head down. Otherwise, you could end up coyote and bug bait on the side of the trail just like your dead friends."

Scared son of a bitch never uttered another word till after we reached civilization again.

8

"BOTH OF YOU'LL BE BARKIN' IN HELL . . ."

We rode into Willow Junction about the time the sun gave up its flaming spot in heaven. Well-established Texas community bustled with visitors from the surrounding hill country. Wagons, buckboards, and horses crowded narrow dirt streets. Women and cherry-cheeked kids in abundance frequented the boardwalks and doorways of every mercantile and shop I could see. Just nothing like the entertainment available for farmers and ranchers during a Saturday night visit to a small town.

Got our animals stabled, and soon found the local lawman's office. Unremarkable building was located about midway of the busy settlement's dusty main street. Unfortunately discovered, right quicklike, that the good folk of that pleasant village had saddled themselves with a badge carrier whose breath carried the powerful odor of hen feathers. Boldly displayed brass plaque on the door declared him as Marshal Ridley Matthews.

Stood at the beer-gutted and red-faced man's litter-covered desk and watched as he disintegrated right before my eyes. With his bootless and poorly socked feet propped in a battered chair, he pawed at an enormous, greasy gut and whined, "What the hell'd you bring 'im here for? If'n he's Nate Coffin's man, I don't want 'im in my jail. Everybody in this whole godforsaken country knows the bunch that follows 'at 'ere wicked son of a bitch will come to my town in force, break him out, and kill us all sure as fat women sweat."

Wasn't in any mood for a debate on the subject, so I snapped back, "You don't have one helluva lot of choice in this matter, Marshal Matthews. Gonna have to put him in one of your empty cells until I can make arrangements for his return to Salt Valley for proper trial and suitable hanging."

Matthews turned, squirted a gob of stringy tobacco juice toward a brimming spittoon from the chewed cigar stub clenched between his yellow-stained teeth, then looked at me like I had three heads and an ear between each pair of eyes.

"Damned if I will," he said. "Maybe I didn't make myself completely understood.

Ain't a livin' soul in these parts that don't know what a murderous monster Nate Coffin is. You force me to put this scum in one of my cells, and Coffin finds out about it, my life won't be worth any more'n a two-ounce lead fishin' sinker."

Dianna had strolled inside with me to inquire as to the whereabouts of a sawbones for MaryLou Wainwright. Face red as scarlet, she pushed around me, placed her hands on the fat slug's desk, and leaned his direction.

Ice in her voice when she snapped, "Ranger Dodge is just trying to be diplomatic. Let me get right to the crux of this matter, Marshal. Hike your lazy rump out of that chair, you big tub of guts, get the keys off the peg behind you, and lock this man up. Or if you'd prefer, I'll put a bullet in him right here and now. Then, when the story gets out that he died in your office, Nate Coffin will pay you a deadly visit for sure."

Matthews came near to choking on the chewed-up cigar stump. His stubby, bootless feet hit the floor as he flopped forward in his chair. Stuttered, "Wha-wha-what the hell d-d-did you just say, woman?"

"Don't tell me you're deaf as well as fat, ugly, and stupid," Dianna shot back. "I said, either lock this murderer up, or you can go buy a shovel and bury him. Your choice. Along with the possibility your wife, if you have one, could well be attending a funeral in the very near future herself."

Nervy gob of spit jumped to his feet, slapped the top of his desk with a sweaty hand, and yelped, "B-b-by God, woman. I'll not listen to such —"

'Fore he knew what happened, the end of his nose was surrounded by the muzzle of her pistol. Gingerly as I could, barely touched her with my finger, and ever so gently pressed the hot-eyed girl's arm back toward her holster. Hell, couldn't allow her to splatter his nose, and most of his brains, all over the jail wall.

Said, "Locals might not take well to us killin' the courageous and renowned Marshal Ridley Matthews, Dianna." Gradually the fire in her eyes came down a scorching notch, and she took a fuming step backward.

Whispered, "Calm down," as she moved away. Turned back to the flabbergasted lawman. "Gonna have to do as the lady says, Marshal. Otherwise, I just might be forced to adopt her hotheaded methods and, trust me, you wouldn't want that."

Matthews looked like a man who'd been slapped in the face with a filthy, puke-dripping, Saturday night bar rag from the busiest saloon in town. His jowly, stubble-covered face twitched around tobacco-stained teeth and lips. "Well, shit, bring 'im on back, by God. But I swear 'fore crucified Jesus, if anything wayward occurs because of this brazen inconvenience, I'm layin' the blame right at your feet. You Rangers need to take up a bit more in the way of polite methods for handlin' your affairs. Cain't just run over folks like this."

Ignored the angry marshal's less than charitable remarks and pushed Tiner to his cage. Smoky wasn't stupid by any means. As Matthews and I headed back into the office, he grabbed the bars, squeezed his face between them, and yelped, "Jist you boys wait till Nate finds out where I am. You law-bringin' sons of bitches won't live any longer'n spit on a stoked-up depot stove in January. Both of you'll be barkin' in Hell soon enough, and I'll be drinkin' tequila at the Los Lobos Cantina over in Uvalde."

His speech bothered me not one whit, but I could tell Tiner's load of horse fritters rattled Matthews, right down to the holes in the toes of his moth-eaten socks. Marshal clumsily wobbled back to his still-warm seat, and slumped into it like a man who'd just been beaten bloody with a fence post sporting a horseshoe nail. Took some doing to get his attention back, but I eventually dragged directions to the office of Willow Junction's local pill roller out of him.

Escorted Dianna and a blank-faced Mrs. Wainwright another few blocks down Front Street toward the easily missed storefront operation of Dr. Hardin Q. Puckett. We shuffled along the boardwalk and, for the first time since we'd found MaryLou Wainwright, I had a chance to notice the amazing contrasts between the two women. Dianna's dark-haired, ruby-lipped, fiery-eyed beauty served as an exact opposite for the shattered Mrs. Wainwright's sandy-haired, pale, vacant-faced appearance.

No way not to feel sorry for the broken lady if you had any knowledge of her blood-saturated recent past. Poor woman's predicament, and the foul murder of Dianna's young son, William, made me all the more determined to see Nate Coffin, and any of his henchmen responsible for such vicious, soulless destruction, swinging from the nearest tree, or spitting blood if they resisted.

Given the disappointment of Willow Junction's less-than-cooperative marshal, the local medicine man turned out much better than I had any right to expect. Far too many of the bone poppers who made their stumbling way to obscure parts of the West drank to excess as a result of being plagued by an unknowable past on the killing fields of Mr. Lincoln's tragic war on the South. Not this one. Gangly, thin as a rail, and nervous in the extreme, Puckett appeared precisely what any person in need would hope for in a pill-wrangling cut-'em-up.

We explained the dreadful circumstances of our appearance. The doc nodded as though he recognized the problem immediately. Placed a skinny arm around the devastated woman's shoulders and guided her to a leather-covered couch in one corner of his office. Long, spiderlike fingers caressed her trembling shoulder as he gently assisted the lady into a reclining position.

"Appears she has involuntarily descended into a profound state of shock," he said. "Her troubled mind, overwhelmed by the brutal circumstances you've recently described, has simply taken a much-needed rest. And will most likely lie dormant until coaxed into properly functioning again."

"I have no idea what that all means, Dr. Puckett. What we have to know is, can you help her?" Dianna's question contained more than a bit of concerned desperation.

"Oh, yes." He turned and gently patted

Dianna's shoulder. "You must not feel compelled to worry yourself overly much, my dear. I'll keep her warm. Prop her feet up. See she gets plenty of liquids and attentive care. With any luck at all, your friend should start coming around in a matter of hours, days perhaps, weeks at the outside."

"That's most encouraging, Doctor," I offered.

He scratched his head for a second, then added, "Yes, but you should also be painfully aware that in some instances these things do take time."

"How much time?" Dianna asked.

"Well, I've seen many past examples of trauma to the wounded mind that refused treatment. 'Course that was during the War of Yankee Oppression — a time of unparalleled human destruction and murderous slaughter. Still, even doctors with considerable training can't accurately foretell the exact outcome for certain. I'd venture an educated guess, though, and say the lady should recover, and be made whole again, in pretty short order."

After seeing to our animals, Dianna and I hit the street in search of a hotel room. We strolled along the boardwalk and she said, "The more I think on it, a night in a real bed would be most agreeable — a skin-singeing bath even more so."

I flicked a furtive glance in the dazzling girl's direction. The overpowering thought of her completely naked body engulfed my every conscious thought.

Of course, we took separate rooms at the Lone Star Hotel and Boarding House located a block away from the jail and across Front Street. Had hoped Dianna's room would be nearer mine, but the desk clerk claimed only limited vacancies at the time. She set up residence near the stairway landing on the second floor, while I had to throw my bedroll in a room several doors farther down the hall. After some consideration, I came to feel that the separation amounted to nothing more than a minor irritation. Wished later I'd thought a bit more on the subject.

Two days after our arrival, Mrs. Wainwright's situation had improved enough that we decided to continue on to Uvalde and points south come the following morning. Had lunch in the hotel with Dianna that afternoon. Lady implored me to bathe myself and shave for a special evening she had planned. Flattered by the mysterious request, I agreed to her terms.

'Course all kinds of wicked thoughts flew through my heaving mind. While our relationship had started out well when we first met, her son's brutal death, and the events surrounding the chase, had thrown water on those initial embers of passion. Couldn't imagine what she intended.

Once Dianna had tended to her twa-let that evening, and freshened herself to the utmost in man-slaying appearance, she tapped on my door. When I opened it, she took my arm and said, "Come along, Ranger Dodge. I've discovered the location of a well-recommended restaurant and would like to buy you dinner."

My God, but she was a glorious thing to look upon. Her dusky beauty entranced me in a way that made it hard to breathe, much less concentrate. From somewhere amidst the load she'd placed on our mule, a flattering, bone-colored dress, accented by a navy-blue shawl trimmed in red, had magically appeared. As my dear ole daddy liked to say, "Lucius, 'at 'ere gal is purdyer'n a fresh-painted wagon."

Did my level best to act surprised and noble. Wasn't difficult. "You needn't do that, Mrs. Savage. I'd be most happy to stand for the two of us to have a good meal."

She looped her arm through mine and pulled me into the hall. "You will do no such thing. Come along now. A grand evening awaits Willow Junction's hungry sojourners at Jewel's Café."

Not often you found a place like Jewel's in the wilds of Texas back in them days. Block or so down from the hotel, the completely out-of-place but elegant restaurant sported starched white tablecloths, vases of handpicked wildflowers, and an actual printed menu that came to the table in a slender, leather-bound jacket.

No blackboard scribblin's in that joint. No sir-ree bob, sir. Hand-lettered in beautifully done script, the heavy vellum bill of fare was clean, crisp, and appeared to change every day. My crude upbringing had me feeling like a rooster at a convention for a pack of wolves.

A smartly dressed waiter, who sported a black bow tie and brocaded silk vest, led the way to a choice table in the farthest corner. Man made quite a production of lighting the candle for us, and poured long-stemmed goblets of red wine. Pointed out his recommendations from the menu, smiled, snapped his polished heels together, then retreated while we made our decisions. Almost made a rough-as-a-cob cowboy like me feel important.

"Well, now, you have surely picked a winner, Mrs. Savage. Can't remember the last time I ate in a place with quite so much snoot value. Perhaps I should have dressed a bit better," I said as we tapped our crystal beakers against one another.

She ignored my self-deprecation, smiled, sipped at her wine, then said, "Most fortunate to find such an amazing establishment, aren't we, Mr. Dodge?"

"Indeed we are."

She leaned forward and spoke in a lowered voice as though intent on telling me a secret. "Wanted you to know how much I appreciate all the help and considerate understanding you've imparted on me, Mr. Dodge. Decided this meal was the best way to demonstrate my deep feelings on the subject."

"Wish you'd call me, Lucius, Mrs. Savage. I do tend to get somewhat discombobulated when you refer to me as though my long-dead father has somehow come back to life and taken a place in the shadows behind me."

Sounded like a schoolteacher when she said, "As you are surely well aware, sir, good manners and the conventions of the day require strict behavior between unmarried adults while in public, Mr. Dodge."

"Well, you're absolutely right, of course. But why don't we make a pact right here and now. In the glow of Jewel's candlelight, or whenever we're not in the company of others, you call me Lucius, and I'll call you Dianna. How does that strike you, Mrs. Savage?"

She smiled. "Perfect, Lucius." She smiled and held her crystal glass out to be struck again.

From that moment on, our relationship changed dramatically and, in my opinion, for the better. For the first time since we'd met, the practice of forced societal formality between us fell away. She became almost girlish in demeanor. And at some point during the course of that astonishing evening, the realization of my simmering attraction to Dianna Savage dropped on me like a Butterfield stage coach. The longer the evening progressed, the more difficult it became for me to concentrate on my meal.

Although probably not on a par with the best offerings of the finer joints in New Orleans, I'm sure, the food at Jewel's ranked several rungs above anything else I'd had in some time past. The main course consisted of fist-sized medallions of beef, bird, and venison that swam in individual pools of mouth-watering sauces. Huge, almost inhuman, slices of buttermilk pie served as dessert. And when we'd finished, the waiter brought the check to the table with a rose, as he said, "For the lady."

Dianna insisted on a promenade around town before we returned to our rooms. She took my arm again. I could feel the warmth of her through my shirt, and found the stunning woman's perfume damned near overpowering. More than once that evening I felt light-headed. As though no longer attached to this earth.

We strolled from one end of Willow Junction's six-block-long Main Street to the other like young lovers. The abbreviated trip lasted barely fifteen minutes. Under an enormous moon, aided by oil lamps and candlelight from behind glass windows in the shops, saloons, and mercantile businesses, everything about our short walk felt right and gloriously comfortable. Finally we made our way up the stairs to her room, and she appeared reluctant to see our evening come to an end.

Upon arrival at her door she turned, squeezed my arm, leaned forward, molded her body to mine, and pressed her lips against my cheek. Felt her warm, scented breath on my ear. She whispered, "I have not forgotten our first evening together. Memories of that initial meeting are with me at every waking moment. Being near you like this imparts the most fervent upheaval in my anxious heart. Soon. Not now, but soon, dear Lucius."

And with that, the most beautiful woman I'd ever known disappeared into the deeper darkness of her chamber. Left me in the rude hallway to contemplate the exhilarating aroma of her perfume. Stood in the intoxicating cloud that came from her body as it swirled around me. Heard the distinctly final sound of the lock as it clicked into place.

God Almighty, felt like I would explode right on the spot. Never thought any woman could have such a profoundly pleasant impact on me. Stumbled to my empty room, and even emptier bed, in a dense fog of unfulfilled desire.

9

". . . MAN'S KNOWN AS A COLD-BLOODED KILLER . . ."

Fell into my narrow, empty bed that fateful night. Lay atop the sheets and couldn't get thoughts of Dianna's passionate, sensuous body pressed against me out of my mind. I had not allowed any woman to have such a profound impact on me since the day I watched Martye McKee ride out of my life and away from the murderous horrors of Sweetwater and the Nightshade clan. Came to the undeniable conclusion that my total discomfort was exactly what the beautiful Mrs. Savage most probably had in mind for me from the start of our splendid evening at Jewel's Café.

Tossed and turned like a bullfrog in a red-hot frying pan. Can't say with any certainty how much time passed before my eyes finally closed. Hotel and street settled down. The entire world finally got quiet. Sleep crept upon me like a nimble-footed thief carrying a sledgehammer.

Middle of the night, awoke to the sound of a gentle, almost unnoticeable, tapping at my door. An appeal delivered with such hesitation, I barely heard it. Snatched the rough portal open, and Dianna fell into my waiting arms.

A trembling hand caressed my cheek and she whispered, "Changed my mind, dear Lucius. It's a woman's privilege, you know. Decided I couldn't wait any longer."

Then, as God is my witness, that bold and beautiful girl locked liquid lips to mine and damned near kissed me inside out. Thought I would burst into scorching flame and be completely consumed right there in the doorway.

Lifted her up in one quick, catlike movement. Pushed the door closed with my foot and carried her to my bed. Tender, inviting arms draped around my neck as we tasted each other again. The heady flavor of her open mouth proved as intoxicating as any powerful liquor. Fingers of fire danced across my shoulders, neck, and around my ears.

Laid her atop a tangled mass of sheets. In a flurry of heated excitement and pent-up lust, we stripped each other naked. A thin sheen covered our overheated bodies. She glittered and glowed in a hazy obscurity provided by the half-light that stole into my window from an enormous moon.

Agile fingers seared a flaming path down my belly and caressed the core of me right there in the semidarkness. Sent me into a shuddering ecstasy unlike anything I'd ever experienced in my entire life.

A whippoorwill, somewhere outside my open window, sang in the shadows as we made love. Immersed in the sweet, violent warmth of loosed passion and vivid arousal, I plunged into her. Immediately lost myself in the uncontrollable inferno. No doubt about it, all those raw feelings and untamed emotions were sparked by Dianna's astonishing beauty the moment we first met.

As I choose to remember our night of unfettered ardor, the firestorm of passionately meshed bodies, and quietly murmured words of affection in my mind, the lovemaking lasted for hours. At some point, spent and exhausted, I must have fallen asleep — perhaps for only a minute.

When I jerked myself awake again, she'd vanished. Gone as though she'd never been there. Nothing left but the sweet, heady odor of musk that lingered on me and my damp, rumpled bedclothes. Came to wonder if the whole encounter had been nothing more than a wildly pleasant fantasy —

an outrageous, vividly realized dream. Stared at the blank ceiling till fatigue came and claimed me again.

Early the next morning, the sound of rough knuckles pounded on my door and snatched me away from astonishing dreams. Dreams I sometimes still have this very day. Raspy voice from the hallway called out, "Ranger Dodge? Are you there, sir? Ranger Dodge, are you awake, sir?"

Made my muddled-headed, bleary-eyed way to the knob and jerked the portal open. Blockheaded feller, who looked like he'd made every effort possible to appear like Marshal Matthews's exact duplicate, stood in the hallway. His deputy's badge was pinned on the wrong side of a greasy leather vest. The faded bib-front shirt beneath smelled from what gave every appearance of months of accumulated sweat, dirt, and grime-impregnated grease.

"Who the hell are you? Better yet, what the hell do you want?" I snapped.

Stupid son of a bitch didn't even react to my mild rebuke. Lamebrained fool had all the outward personality of a stick of stove wood. Started talking like some kind of mechanical music box. "Name's Porter Atwood, Ranger." He made a halfhearted motion at his badge. That's when I noticed one point of the star was broken off. "Deputy Marshal Porter Atwood."

"Well, you've answered one question. Second one's still the same, Deputy Atwood. What the hell do you mean wakin' me up this ungodly time of morning?"

Hooked his meaty thumbs behind filth-encrusted suspenders, grinned like a tubby possum eating peaches, and proudly declared, "Marshal sent me over. Always do what the marshal says. Yessir. Always do."

Had begun to feel that I'd been awakened by the village idiot. "Why?"

"Whaddaya mean, Ranger?"

"Look, Atwood. Want you to think about my next question very carefully. I'm only gonna ask you once. Why did Marshal Matthews send you here to wake me from a sound sleep?"

For about the count of three he looked like a Hidalgo County brush popper who'd just woke up and discovered a tarantula the size of a pullet in his boot. After several seconds of puzzlement, some kind of light went on behind his heavy-lidded eyes and he said, "Oh, Marshal said as how he shore could use yore help, if'n you've got the time and inclination."

"Help doin' what?"

Well, he looked at me with all the confusion of a woodpecker in a petrified forest. Shook my head and said, "Go back to the jail and tell him I'll be down in about fifteen minutes. Think you can do that without gettin' lost along the way?"

He rubbed tobacco juice dribbles off his nasty chin with a stained shirtsleeve and nodded like a drunk duck. "Hell, yes, I can do'er. Ain't nothin' to it, Ranger."

"Head on out then, Deputy. I'll be down shortly." Poor churnhead nodded like he understood. 'Bout the time he got to the end of the hall I called out, "Remember now, try not to get lost." Certain he didn't understand the joke either time, but at least he grunted like he heard me.

Got myself in no hurry. Dressed and armed up in my own sweet time. Passed the entrance to Dianna's room on the way out. Wanted desperately to see her. Hold her. Hear her voice again. Smell the heat and fire of her.

Stopped and quietly pressed my ear to the closed door. No movement inside. Considered knocking. At the very least I should have let her know what had just transpired, but thought better of such action when I checked my two-dollar Ingersoll pocket watch and realized just how early the hour truly was.

Stepped into Ridley Matthews's office to find the portly marshal, Atwood, and another deputy who appeared even shorter on thinker-box filler than either of his fellows. Tall, thin, and hawk-nosed, the unnamed lawman gave the red-faced appearance of someone who spent way too much time in one of the local whiskey emporiums with a dipper of stump squeezin's attached to a trembling, clawlike hand.

Matthews hopped up from his desk like a man who'd been struck by lightning, or caught doing something he shouldn't. "Coffee, Ranger?" he asked, and gifted me with a blazingly counterfeit smile.

Seemed an odd response to my expected entrance. Puzzled me some at first, but I accepted the tin cup and flopped into the only empty chair. Figured they were all idiots just this side of being institutionalized in the nearest insane asylum and had to be humored.

Matthews resumed his well-worn seat and assumed a surprisingly officious air. "You know, Ranger Dodge," he droned, "few years ago a feller named Herman Wallace ranched some out on Turkey Creek. Got into a dispute over borrowed cattle. Seems Wallace harbored the belief as how a neighbor, Simp Richards, spent most of his time throwin' a wide loop on animals what belonged to the owners of surrounding ranches. Guess one day ole Herman finally got all he wanted. Rode over to Simp's place and shot the man dead as a rotten fence post. Then, Herman went to runnin' and hidin'. Nobody around these parts would admit to havin' seen the man since. Mighty frustratin' for a lawman, as you might well guess."

"And what, Marshal Matthews, has any of your profoundly sad tale about rustlin' and murder got to do with gettin' me out of bed at the butt crack of dawn?"

His confused eyes swirled around in a beet-red face before he said, "Well, 'pears the murderous son of a bitch decided to return and, from all indications, has taken up residence in his old ranch house out Turkey Creek way. Just wondered if you might be willing to come along with us. Help make the arrest."

Couldn't believe my ears. "You mean to tell me Willow Junction's three fearless, redoubtable, and mostly stalwart lawdogs can't get this job done on their own?"

Matthews dismissed my obvious slur with the wave of a nervous hand. "Herman Wallace is widely known as a cold-blooded killer, Dodge. More trouble than we can handle, to tell the absolute truth. Don't have many killers here'bouts, or a famed Texas Ranger available to offer aid and assistance in such matters."

"Hell, Marshal, hate to be the one to point out the obvious again, but there's three of you boys. Ain't that enough?"

"Look, Dodge, sad truth is us town boys don't really have much in the way of experience when it comes to dealin' with brazen murderers. You got to admit, this ain't Fort Worth, Dallas, or one of them Kansas railhead towns, like Wichita or Abilene. They's mostly nothin' but farmers and ranchers here'bouts. Not many man killers. None but Herman Wallace since I've been in office."

Racked my brain, but couldn't readily figure any way to weasel out of his appeal. Man had politely requested assistance and, in obedience to my sworn oath, I felt compelled to comply.

Matthews wanted to leave as soon as possible. Told him I'd be glad to help, and headed directly for the livery. Met back up with him and Atwood about fifteen minutes later.

"Where's your other deputy?" I asked.

Matthews leaned on his saddle horn, threw a nervous glance over his shoulder, then said, "You mean Jiles?"

150

"That his name?"

"Yeah. Pinky Jiles. Well, he's fine enough here in town, but 'bout as worthless as half a haircut for any kind of real action. Man can't hit his own ass with a set of antlers and five jabs." He and Atwood laughed at his lame joke. "Even worse with a pistol. Main reason I asked for your help, Dodge. Besides, I cain't just go off and leave all our fine upstandin' citizens completely bereft of at least somethin' akin to law. Just never know what might come to pass during my absence."

The revelation that Deputy Pinky Jiles was about as useful as a screen door in the bottom of a rowboat didn't come as any great surprise. However, I cared not one whit about leaving the town, and especially Dianna, in the care of a man not worth his feed. Ugly threat of Nate Coffin, or any number of his henchmen, making an unexpected raid loomed large in my mind as we spurred our animals and headed for Turkey Creek.

Much to my increasing vexation, Willow Junction's chief lawman had failed to let me know, in advance, that the Wallace spread lay out in the briars and brambles nearly thirty miles from town. After we'd traveled over rolling hills for nigh two hours, I got to wondering just how long the trip would take.

"How much farther, Marshal Matthews?" I asked.

"Oh, not more'n five miles. Should be there in another forty-five minutes, maybe an hour at the most. Ain't that far away."

Whole irritating situation had begun to get under my skin by that point. Went to thinking as how I should have stopped at the hotel desk and at least left word for Dianna as to my intentions. Now the unplanned trip was taking much longer than I expected. Virtually all the law in that part of the country had vacated town, left it in the care of a known drunk and idler. Man very likely couldn't have saved himself from any problem much more threatening than which brand of tarantula killer to swill down first.

About the time I had given up ever arriving at the Herman Wallace spread, we stopped under a sheltering stand of cottonwoods on the bank of what Matthews proclaimed was Turkey Creek. Heat forced me to remove my hat and cool an aching head from a canteen. Stepped down and refilled with clear, running water from the rocky stream.

Matthews pointed to a spot a bit farther up and said, "Ranch building is just over yonder, Dodge. You can barely make it out 'cause of all these trees here on the creek. Herman built as close to water as he could get. Live oaks all around the main house as well. Bit tight in this spot here, but plenty of cover provided by several sizable boulders all around the place. Should be able to sneak up on him unawares. Have the murdering skunk under the gun and in our custody plenty quick."

Pulled my big popper and strapped a bandolier of shotgun shells over my pistol belt. Neither of the other lawmen bothered with any kind of additional weapon. Stuck with a handgun each. Being as we'd made the trip in search of a known man killer, it puzzled me some that they didn't at least carry their rifles. Way I had it figured, both would have been a hell of a lot better off toting a shotgun. Tied the animals in scrubby bushes and silently picked our way from spot to spot for the rest of the way.

Stand of trees bled out on a deep, grass-covered field. Sun-dried, knee-high grass had overtaken what had once been a rail corral. No animals of any kind in evidence as I could detect. Low log-and-plank main house had suffered from considerable neglect, as had a smaller cabinlike structure formerly used by hired hands.

Situated amidst several large boulders, the compound of main house, split-rail corrals, and outbuildings lay at the back of the meadow between a number of massive live oaks and our spot near the creek. Front door stood ajar on the owner's main residence. Appeared to have been ripped from its leather hinges. Roof of the barn had caved in and, if anyone had asked me at the time, I would have vowed the entire place was totally abandoned. Should have listened to what my whispering sense of right and wrong tried to tell me.

Without any warning, an uncomfortable feeling that something about the entire situation rang false fell on me like a frozen steer dropped from the rafters of Heaven. As Boz might have said, felt like we'd done gone and started chopping on the wrong tree.

Matthews quietly motioned us all into defensive positions. I took a spot to his right, behind what was left of a water trough near the crumbling corral. Atwood stayed attached to his leader like a scared kid. The pair of them hid behind a wagon-sized boulder about sixty feet from the front entrance.

Had barely got myself settled when the marshal yelled, "Herman Wallace, I command you, in the name of the law, to present yourself for immediate arrest in the killing of Simp Richards."

Nothing. Not one sound. No movement. So he tried again with the same exhortation. That time he added as how we'd blast the bejabbers out of ole Herman if the murderous neighbor killer refused to show himself, and damned quick.

Still got no response. Place was quieter than a snowstorm at midnight. Glanced over to where Matthews and Atwood cowered. Near as I could tell, neither man appeared to have any intention of taking the bull by the tail and really confronting the nasty situation.

Cocked both barrels on my short-barreled blaster, and waited while Matthews yelped out his ultimatum one final time. Nothing. Not a single sound in reply. Appeared as how any action from our side would have to start with me. Got myself bucked up to make a run for the door. Figured I'd go in blasting. Clear the main room out with both barrels of buckshot, throw the big shooter aside, and finish up with my pistols.

Soon as I stood and exposed myself, a hailstorm of bullets, from behind, fell all around me. Partially rotted boards of the trough, where I'd just been hiding, burst into shards of flying splinters.

Whirlwinds of dust squirted up around my feet as I turned and heeled it for the open door of the main house. Red-clawed, yellow-toothed death chased me and peppered my footfalls every step of the way. Hot lead buzzed past my flaming ears like angry hornets.

Terrible thought crossed my heaving mind 'bout then. For the first time in my riotous life as a Texas Ranger, wondered if I would make it to safety alive.

10

"... I DONE BEEN SHOT BLIND."

Still think on that frightful dash as the longest twenty steps I've ever had to run in my entire life. Don't have the slightest recollection of how I dodged a sizzling curtain of hot lead that zipped past my ears, singed smoking spots in the sleeves of my shirt, knocked the hat off my head, and destroyed the heel on one of my boots. Heavenly intervention's the only explanation I've ever managed to come up with.

Tried to count the shooters as I hoofed it. Figured as how there had to have been at least four men slinging lead my direction — not well, but they sure as the devil poured it on heavy. Hell of it was Matthews and Atwood appeared to be leading the gutless attack. Poor back-shooting, dumb sons of bitches had drawn me into a clumsy and ill-conceived ambush. Felt like a complete fool for having fallen for their ham-fisted ruse.

Crashed through the disintegrating ranch

building's front entrance. Landed hard on the dirt floor littered with tree limbs and trash. Cyclonic storm cloud of blue whistlers chewed the framework around the sagging doorway to bits, kicked up more dirt on all sides of me, and chiseled deep pits into the crumbling cabin's back wall. Rolled and got to my feet in a heartbeat.

Headed for the back of the tumbled-down building fast as I could leg it. Blasted the partially closed rear entrance to smithereens with both barrels of buckshot. Wood splinters filled the air like a swarm of lightning bugs on a hot summer night. Smashed my way through the pellet-riddled planks in a whirlwind of rotten wood fragments and flying dust. Thanks to a merciful God, my less-than-intelligent ambushers hadn't thought far enough ahead to cover the rear entrance.

Turned toward the corner nearest the abandoned corral in a combination run, stumble, and fall for the God-sent shelter provided by one of those gigantic live oaks. Tree stood about midway of the rotting split-rail horse pen. Breeched my weapon and reloaded as I burned boot leather.

Dropped into a hollowed-out depression behind the tree. Surrounded by twisted, ropelike, ground-level roots, the life-saving dent in the earth's ancient hide provided decent protection. More importantly, I had a right fine view of the boulder where Willow Junction's traitor of a marshal and his chief deputy hid their sorry, back-shooting selves. Cowardly scum held their pistols above the rock's shelter and fired blindly. Fact that either man managed to hit the house left me much amazed.

Took almost a minute to finally pick out three other shooters. Sorry, low-life no-accounts lurked in the trees. Spent a bit thinking on my somewhat precarious situation. Came to the discomforting conclusion that the unknown gunmen must have followed us all the way from town, or fell in behind along the trail.

But that realization came nowhere near to the worst of it. Made me madder than a rained-on rooster to know that my fellow lawmen had led me into a trap, and then betrayed me like a pair of slimy Judases. Even worse, those same men were now locked in a deadly attempt to take my life.

Pulled my cavalry-model Colt from the holster I wore at my back. Seven-and-a-half-inch barrel on the gun provided considerable more distance, and accuracy, than the two sheriff's models I carried on one hip and as a belly gun.

Near as I could tell, none of the ambushers had as yet spotted me in my new and much safer position. But I knew beyond any doubt, once I fired the first shot, they'd all ferret out my hidey-hole and swing another blistering wall of lead my direction.

While they blasted away at nothing, I picked out the one gunny that appeared the most careless of the group. Nervy feller appeared to believe himself bulletproof. Stepped from behind his sheltering tree and blazed away one time too many. Stupid gomer looked more like a farmer than an assassin. Dropped the hammer on him first instant he gave me a really good target to shoot at.

Big .45 slug caught him dead center. Must have really surprised the dry-gulchin' skunk. Well-placed shot knocked the back-shooting snake ass over teakettle. He screeched, flopped around, and sprayed blood from the geyser in his chest. Splattered everything within ten feet. That single, surprising turn of events stunned all them ambushers into several moments of head-scratching inactivity.

Tried to nail the man nearest the one I'd just dropped the instant he poked his head out just right. Might not have hit him, but did send a nasty wad of tree bark and splinters into his eyes. Way he hooted and hollered, you'd of thought I could just as well have killed him too. Everything got real quiet for more than a minute after that.

Then, from the safety of his sheltering boulder, I heard Matthews yell, "We cain't let you live, Dodge. Guess you know that, don't you?"

Hollered back, "You're ridin' down the wrong trail, Matthews. Bad decision on your part all around. This ugly mess is gonna end up costin' you your life."

"Cain't go back to town 'less you're dead. Some of Coffin's men arrived last night. Came by the jail."

"So?"

"They'd done went and took my wife in hand. Holdin' her prisoner, Dodge. Said they's gonna kill her if'n you ain't rubbed out. Woman's a fifty-year-old innocent in all this. She don't deserve to die over the killin' of a child in a pissant place like Salt Valley."

"Most cases, I'd probably agree with that sentiment, Matthews, but this is one hell of a bad way to handle the situation."

"Ranger, you brought the whole vile mess on us when you stopped in my town and locked Tiner up, you arrogant son of a bitch. I warned you then as how bad things could fall out if Nate Coffin discovered what you'd gone and done. Man's nefarious. He knows everthang as happens in these parts 'fore they even take place. Good God, but you folks from up north are stupid beyond reasonable belief. Just ain't got no idea of how deadly bad our collective situation is down this way."

Had a serious problem believing that faulty reasoning could lead a man like Matthews into blackhearted, back-shooting murder. "You think killin' a commissioned Ranger is gonna solve your problem, Marshal? Really believe my death will save your wife and the town?"

"Figured this here was as good a ruse as any to get a man of your reputation out away from witnesses. Once we kill you, I've been assured this mess can be worked out."

Hurried to reload all my spent cartridges while he jawed. "Murder me out here, bury the corpse, and no one would ever know the difference. That the plan?"

"Yeah. Somethin' like that."

"You are aware, of course, that Mrs. Savage would bring the entirety of Company B down on you. Boz Tatum is on his way to find me, and he will see you in the ground no matter what the outcome here today. You know all that too, don't you?"

A moment of silence passed. Then he said the one thing that lit a fire under me like nothing else could have. "Ain't no problem with the woman, Dodge. Coffin's men back in town shoulda done took care of her — by now."

At first, my head went to spinning. Thought for a second I might black out. Took about another second for the shock to pass and for a killing rage the likes of which I'd never known to take its place.

Peeked around the tree. Found all three of the remaining shooters in a heartbeat. Poor cowboy with the eyeful of splinters was still howling. That left Matthews, his stupid, potbellied deputy, and one unknown Coffin gunny who could still function. Checked my hip and belly pistols for quickest access, cocked both barrels of the shotgun, and pulled the cavalry Colt. Stepped from the safety of the live oak. Big blaster in one hand, pistol in the other.

"Come on out, boys. Y'all start walkin' this way and we'll get this settled right here and now. Ain't got no time to waste. You wanted a killin'? Well, get up on your hind legs and come get it."

Must have scared Deputy Atwood slap out of his feeble mind. He started running and hollering like something insane. Flew right past Coffin's last functioning back shooter, who jumped from behind his tree and fired my direction — just as a shot from my pistol hit Atwood between the shoulder blades.

Outlaw's bullet got my attention when it scorched a bloody trench through my shirt and along my right side. Ambusher instantly knew he'd missed, and grabbed his pistol with both hands in an effort to steady his next shot. My shotgun blast knocked him out of his boots. Looked right odd flying through the air with sockless, naked feet hanging out of shredded britches legs.

Hoofed my way to the boulder and found Ridley Matthews cowering on the ground like some kind of sniveling, little ole widow woman. He threw his weapon away, and whimpered. Used the muzzle of my big popper under his trembling, puppy-dog chin to urge him up. Tears streamed down the coward's dirt-streaked face.

He held shaky hands in the air and whined, "God Almighty, don't kill me, Dodge. Wouldn't have had no truck with any of this crew, or their despicable plans, if not for my wife. Ain't no killer. You have to know that, don't you?"

Pushed the shotgun's muzzle into his gut and snapped, "No, I don't. Spotted you for a snake the first time we met. You've done nothing with this cowardly action but confirm my suspicions. Now, what in the blue-eyed hell did you mean when you said Coffin's men should have already taken care of Mrs. Savage?"

"I ain't for certain."

"Well, unless you want to die where you stand, you'd damned sure better get somewhere close to certain. If anything wayward has happened to that lady, I'll personally skin you alive and make tobacco pouches for all my friends from your extensive hide."

He glanced around like a man so bewildered his mind had ceased to function. "Jesus, Dodge, you done went and kilt Porter. Poor feller wouldn't a-hurt a fly."

"If that's the way you feel, you shouldn't have brought him into this, Matthews. Any man starts shooting at me from behind had best get ready to meet Jesus, 'cause I'm gonna send him there quicker'n double-geared lightning. Could well consider yourself damned lucky I haven't killed you — yet." Thought the stricken man would pass out. Turned white as a freshly washed sheet. Eyes rolled back up in his head and he went to shaking as though in the throes of a severe case of the ague.

Finally got control of himself again and said, "Honest to God, Dodge, I ain't sure about the woman. Coffin's bunch wanted to know where she was. Said I didn't have to worry none about her. Said Coffin wanted her soon as they could get her back to him. That's all I know. I swear it."

"Come with me." Grabbed the worthless scum by the neck and pushed him toward the blinded gunman.

Sad case, that one. My shot, which should have taken the sneaky ambusher's head off, made one hell of a mess. Clumps of bloody wood splinters protruded from both his cheeks and eyeballs. Bullet had traveled on and put a crease in his skull along a path over a notched right ear. All apparent evidence indicated you could make a pretty safe bet he would never see again from at least one of those badly damaged orbs.

Pushed Matthews onto a log seat, pointed at him, and said, "You make a move my direction, you son of a bitch, and I swear 'fore Jesus, it'll be your last."

Propped the shotgun against the wounded ambusher's covering tree, and pulled one of my pistols. Grabbed Coffin's blinded gunfighter by his shirt. Kneeled down and got right in his bloody, splinter-riddled face and growled, "Where'd them others back in Willow Junction take the woman?" In the back of my mind, I figured if I rushed into the problem, without some idea of the lay of the land, Dianna could very surely get killed graveyard dead. Needed as much information as the sightless lowlife could provide.

Like a child frightened of invisible, unknowable creatures in the dark, he held hands that trembled in front of his punctured face and eyes and sobbed. "Oh, Sweet God, mister. Think I done been shot blind. Are you the man what done the deed?"

"Sure enough, I'm the one."

Through quaking fingers he had grit enough to say, "Well, goddamn you, sir. Be a cold day in Satan's fiery pit 'fore I'll tell you one damned thing."

"Mighty nervy for a man who can't see." Shot him in the foot, just to get his undivided attention. Not sure who screamed the loudest, the one I blasted, or Willow Junction's panicked marshal.

Matthews must have thought I intended to plug him next. He dropped onto his fat stomach and screeched, "Jesus Christ on a crutch, Dodge. Dear Sweet Lord, you've already taken the man's eyes. Why don't you just go ahead and kill 'im?"

Blind, foot-shot gunman passed out cold as a log-splitting wedge in February. Got down and slapped his cheeks good and proper till he came around. Drew right up in the gunny's pain-contorted face and said, "Come on back to us, now. Wake up. Snap out of it. What's your name, mister?"

"Aw-w-w-w, Jesus save me," he moaned, and almost fainted a second time.

"Don't go out on me again now. Stay awake. Need some information." Slapped him some more.

"Torque, Torque, Ranger. Name's Joe Torque. Please stop hittin' on me. Moves these damned splinters 'round. Hurts like seven kinds of hell."

"Manners. I like that. Well, Joe Torque, you're messed up pretty good. Bleedin' somethin' fierce from the foot shot. Big .45 hole's pumpin' your life out on the ground to beat the band. All the wounds to the face and eyes are right scary-lookin'. Way I've got it figured, you'll never see again if we can't get you back to the doc soon — maybe not even then. Pretty sure you're gonna be walkin' on a cane for the rest of your life 'cause of that damaged foot."

Torque completely lost it. Went to screeching, "Oh, God. Oh, God. Oh, God."

"Stop howlin' and pay attention." Slapped the back of his head. "Need you to think on what I'm about to say." Jerked his shirtfront again. "You listenin' to me, Joe?"

"Uh, Sweet Merciful Jesus, yeah, yeah, I hear you."

"Now, would you like to try for an amputated arm as the result of being shot in the elbow?" Pressed the pistol muzzle against the knobby joint. Man damn near passed out again. "One-eyed, limpin' cripple, maybe one-armed. Hell, you're gonna be a mess, if you don't do some mighty fast talkin', Joe."

"Oh, God, I'm beggin'. Don't shoot me again. Just gimme a chance to think. Tell you anything you want to know. All you gotta do is ask. Ain't gonna get disrespectful again. I swear it, Ranger. I swear it."

"Now that's better, much better. Question hasn't changed. You don't even have to think about it, but I'll ask again real slow, being as how you done went and got yourself hurt and all. Where-did-your-friends-take-the-woman?"

Never hesitated the second time around. "Uvalde, so far as I know. Maybe from there on to Coffin's ranch, but I cain't say for absolute sure."

"You have any idea as to Coffin's intent with the woman?"

Wavered a bit on that one. Swung his bloody head back and forth for a few seconds as though puzzled. "He said we shouldn't hurt her any more'n necessary. Said he wanted her undamaged. Said he could get more for her that way."

Answer surprised me a bit. "What the hell does 'get more for her' mean?"

"Hell, I ain't no gypsy mind reader." He grabbed at the air several times. Finally found my hand. "Don't shoot me, please. Swear on my sainted mother's grave, I ain't for certain sure. Maybe he plans on sellin' that gal. Yeah, probably sell her down in Mexico. That's the ticket."

Stood me up like he'd slapped me in the face. "Sell her? Where would Coffin *sell* an American woman?"

Torque must have realized his advantage and brightened up a bit. Seemed a subject he favored. "Aw, you know. Piedras Negras. Nuevo Laredo. Zaragosa. Nate knows lots of shady types down that way. Kind what buy and sell folks. Especially good-lookin' gringo women. Always a market for one of them kind."

"What people does he know?"

"You've seen the kind I mean. Men who'd pay a handsome price for a white woman what hadn't seen much in the way of hard use. Kind that didn't look like she'd been rode hard and put up wet. Kind like 'at 'ere Savage woman. Prime stuff, from what I seen."

Blood loss must've got him. Of a sudden, his head flopped to one side. Knelt down again and shook him so hard his teeth rattled. "Wake up, damn you. Can't die yet, Joe. We ain't finished." Slapped him again. "Don't leave me. Not now, Joe, come on back."

Sorry slug's head lolled from side to side as he finally began to regain consciousness. His splinter-filled eyes swam in bloody circles. Suddenly he latched onto my arm again. Said, "Am I dead? Oh, God, I still cain't see. Is this Heaven? Are you God?"

Question brought me up short. "No, I'm not God, Joe. But I am the man who'll send you to Him if you've lied to me. Swear it on my father's grave."

To my shock, and stunned amazement, the wounded brigand made an odd strangling sound, went rigid under my hand, then collapsed in a limp, bloody heap. Placed a finger against the big vein in his neck. Couldn't find anything in the way of a pulse.

Matthews jumped to his feet, snatched his hat off, and threw it on the ground. Went to pulling at his hair. "He's dead, ain't he. Sweet Jesus. God have mercy. When Nate Coffin finds out what happened here, my wife's life won't be worth a bucket of cold horse piss."

"Shut the hell up," I snapped.

He flopped down on the log again, and howled like a lost dog. "They'll kill my poor wife 'fore we can get back to town. Sweet Jesus, told you, Dodge — you coldhearted son of a bitch. Never should've come to my town draggin' that skunk Tiner. Damn you and all those like you."

Holstered the pistol, and released my grip on the dead outlaw's shirtfront. Turned and slapped the blathering Matthews on the back of his head hard enough to make the wax pop out of his ears. Grabbed up my shotgun by the barrel and said, "Stop babblin' like an idiot. Only people who know what happened out here are you and me. Get to your horse. If we can surprise them boys as have your wife, we should be able to save her."

Once we'd rounded up our animals and got saddled, I shook my finger in his face and said, "Put the spur to your beast. Make sure you stay ahead of me. Kick hard, Marshal. Don't make me have to go around you. If I have to pass, I'll leave your corpse in the dirt behind me."

Must have scared Willow Junction's gutless lawdog damned near to death. Matthews pushed that poor horse like yellow-eyed demons chased the two of them. As a consequence, we made it back to town in what had to be record time.

In a stroke of uncommonly good fortune for the marshal, the remainder of Coffin's bunch had already pulled up stakes and headed out of town. The very portly, blubbering Mrs. "Marshal" Matthews appeared no worse for her frightening ordeal.

While the relieved lawman commiserated with his distraught wife, I headed for the hotel. Stomped up to the desk and asked as to the welfare of Mrs. Savage. Red-faced clerk stuttered around a bit, and then said, "Sh-sh-she's gone. She left, Ranger Dodge."

"What the hell do you mean she left?"

"Came down the stairs yesterday several hours after your departure. Escorted by two rough-lookin' men. They left." He scratched his head. "It's that simple."

"What two men?"

"Can't say with any degree of certainty, sir."

"Well, why don't you try and make an educated guess."

"To tell the truth, sir, I think they might've been members of the Nate Coffin gang."

For about five seconds, all the air got sucked out of my entire world. An unseen hand jerked the earth from beneath my feet. Limp legs almost dropped me to the floor in a heap. Felt hot all over and a sheet of sickly sweat drenched me from head to foot. A multitude of flame-tinged feelings burned their way through my brain in a raging forest fire of horrific thoughts. I couldn't imagine what it meant, or would mean in the future.

Of a sudden, my mind lit up with each and every time we'd been together, or touched. Vivid memories of the heat and fire of her as she leaned against me flashed through my heart and set my soul aflame.

Ran a quaking hand over my sweaty brow and said, "Might've been? What do you mean by that?"

He ducked his head, swayed back and forth on unsteady feet. Fidgeted with the hotel ledger. Leaned over, cupped his hand, and whispered, "Them fellers said they'd come back and kill everyone in town, Ranger. Start with me, if'n I said anything amiss. Sorry, but all I know about the lady is that she's no longer here. She left."

Slapped the top of his desk in frustration. "Damn," I snapped.

He stepped back, held a hand up as if in defense. "One thing I did notice. Appeared the lady resisted. She'd been roughed up a mite. Not much. But enough as you could tell it."

Figured he'd given me all I could expect.

Frustrated with what I perceived would most likely prove a total collective memory loss and widespread gutlessness on the citizenry's part, I headed directly for Willow Junction's jail. By the time I got there, my anger had doubled, then tripled.

Thundered through the door of Marshal Matthew's calaboose ready to kill anyone inside. Surprised the hell out of me when I found Boz Tatum seated behind the local lawman's desk.

My partner unlimbered his lanky frame, leaned onto the office chair's arms with his elbows, grinned, and said, "Well, I'll just be surely damned. You know, for the first time since we met, that fateful day back in the White Elephant Saloon when ole Peaches McCabe tried to kill the hell out of me, do believe you actually look surprised, Lucius 'By God' Dodge."

"Mighty good to see you, Boz. You don't know how good," I said.

He placed a burning panatela on the edge of a tin plate full of tobacco ashes, and stood as I stomped over to him. "Sweet Jesus, Lucius, wish they was one of them travelin' photographers 'round this buffalo waller of a town somewheres to record this singular and marvelous event. Would love to have a tintype of it to carry 'round in my pocket."

11

". . . AIN'T WORTH A BUCKET OF COLD SNAKE PISS . . ."

Thanks to Boz Tatum's welcome appearance, my flagging spirits soared. He brought something I sorely needed — hope. Held out my hand and said, "God, but it's damn fine to have you back again, amigo. How long you been in town?"

He dismissively waved at the air with one paw and shook mine with the other. "Well, I hit the trail runnin' soon as I got your wire. After damned near exhausting virtually all my extensive trackin' skills to run you down, I arrived just before noon today."

"Notice anything amiss?"

"Found this here pissant town in one hell of an uproar. God Almighty, but gettin' information out of folks around these parts is harder'n holdin' a handful of tadpoles. Finally weaseled it out of a reluctant storekeeper that you were still alive and somewhere nearby. He also intimated as how some of Nate Coffin's bunch done showed up. Guess them boys musta just about scared the bejabbers out of damned near everyone available."

"According to the hotel clerk, the sons of bitches took Mrs. Savage, Boz," I blurted out.

"The hell you say." Man looked like I had slapped his jaw hard enough to make his ears ring.

"Just found out for certain sure myself. 'Course I suspected as much, given what I'd already forced out of Marshal Matthews earlier today."

"That a fact? Where you boys been anyway?"

"Out in the briars and brambles on a wild-goose chase. Appears Coffin's bunch scared the bejabbers out of Matthews by threatenin' to kill the man's wife. They wanted me gone, or dead, so he came up with a cock-and-bull story 'bout needin' my help. Got me out in the tall and uncut as part of an underhanded effort to kill me. Suffice it to say, his poorly executed back shootin' didn't work."

Blood welled up in my friend's neck and spread to his cheeks. "Well, by God," he snorted, "hope you sent his sorry hide to flamin' perdition on an outhouse door."

Shook my head. "Threatened to do exactly

that. Had to keep him alive, though. Once the blastin' ended, decided I would need the craven snake to find out exactly what was goin' on."

He snatched his smoke up and took a deep drag, blew a heavy cloud toward the ceiling, picked a sprig of tobacco off his lip, then said, "You cut off anything important belongin' to the dirty polecat in that effort?"

"No, but after a bit of indirect persuasion, he did come across with the reason for all this."

"And what might that be?"

"Seems Coffin's wicked purpose was the same as it's always been — to get his already blood-soaked hands on Mrs. Savage for killin' his worthless brother. Wounded outlaw I spoke with expressed the opinion that she'll most likely be sold to flesh peddlers down Mexico way. Guess Coffin discovered his assassins failed in their Salt Valley mission. Wouldn't surprise me none if I discovered Marshal Matthews is the man responsible for getting word to him. Threatened to kill the worthless skunk. Guess I should have made good on it but, hell, he ain't worth the expense of wastin' good powder and shot on."

Boz smoothed his drooping moustache with one hand, then took a deep-lunged hit off his cigar. "Sweet Jesus, Lucius. That's bad news indeed, my friend. Couldn't have figured on anything like that since my recent arrival. Naturally, came directly to this office after my discussion with the storekeeper. Place was emptier'n an Arizona water gourd in August. Been sittin' here at the marshal's desk ever since I got in."

Got creeping gooseflesh up and down my spine. "You haven't seen a deputy named Jiles?"

"Nope. Ain't seen nobody, as a pure matter of fact. Town's been quieter than snowflakes fallin' on a feather bed. This feller Jiles supposed to be around here somewheres?"

All at once I felt as though an icy chill hit me right between the shoulder blades. "Have you been back in the cell block, Boz?"

Virtually in unison, we turned toward the slab-thick door. In a somewhat quizzical tone, Boz said, "Had no reason to go back there. No one called out or nothin'. Been nappin' in this chair almost all afternoon. Knew for certain your trail ended right here in town. Figured you'd show up sooner or later."

By that point we had both moved to the stout, wooden cell block entrance door and

179

pulled cocked pistols. An iron-barred window in the center of the door revealed little inside. Raised the metal latch, and the heavy door easily swung open unimpeded.

Gingerly eased inside and past the first three cells — empty, all of them. But the last one contained a gruesome surprise Coffin's lackeys had left behind. Beneath a rough blanket, as though asleep on his side, we found the bullet-riddled corpse of Deputy Pinky Jiles.

"Wonder if this message is for you, Lucius, or the town's marshal."

"Most likely for Matthews. Way Coffin's killers had it figured, I should be dead by now. Be willin' to place bets this is a warnin' for the marshal. There's someone missing from back here as well."

"Who?"

"Yellow-belly named Smoky Tiner. He was one of the men who shot up Mrs. Savage's house and killed young William. Coffin's men must have taken him with 'em."

Boz scratched his chin and said, "Well, we cain't do nothin' 'bout the one that's gone, or for this poor feller here either, for that matter. You reckon there's any more like this dead 'un hidden in different spots around town, Lucius?"

"Jesus, that's a frightenin' thought. Don't know. Matthews claimed his wife was threatened with murderous mayhem if he didn't cooperate. Left him with the lady not more'n fifteen minutes ago. She appeared just fine as frog hair to me."

Boz took me by the arm and led the way back to the outer office. He gently pushed the cell block door closed before he said, "When do you want to get after them as took Mrs. Savage?"

"Soon as we can get provisioned, loaded, and ready. Much as I feel emotionally compelled to burn leather, there's no beneficial point I can think of for leaving this late in the day. See to everything we'll need. Head south at first light. Don't like givin' the brigands any more head start than necessary, but it'll be pitch-dark in less than half an hour. Might as well get a good meal and a comfortable night's sleep."

That bloody day turned into one of the most restless nights of my life. Couldn't find the path to peaceful slumber, no matter how diligently I searched. My chaotic mind raced with terrible images of a captured Dianna Savage, and burned with unquenchable, fiery thoughts of how I'd failed her.

Never should have left the woman alone, I told myself. Should have known, or at least suspected, the risks and consequences. Flogged my tortured sense of right and wrong with the possibility that her captors had already abused her in unspeakable ways in spite of what Joe Torque had told me. Made silent promises to God that if I could retrieve her unharmed, I'd make amends for my past transgressions.

When all that failed to satisfy my rebellious conscience, pledged retribution of Biblical proportions on those I would soon determine guilty of any mistreatment of Dianna — whether real or imagined. By the time the sun finally came up again, I was bed-weary and damned near exhausted.

Boz took note of my unsettled state of mind. As the sun gradually brought orange-tinted light to our efforts at preparation, he pulled at the cinch strap on his saddle and said, "Let not your soul be troubled, my good friend. We'll have the lady back, as God is my witness, I swear it." It was perhaps the most heartfelt and serious statement I'd ever heard from him up till then.

Climbed on Grizz and said, "Not too worried about getting her back, Boz. But must admit I am some concerned as to what kind of physical and mental condition she'll be in when we do."

We headed south and west for Uvalde at

near breakneck speed. Boz ran ahead and searched for the brigands' trail. I fell back and led the mule. Caught up with my friend at varying intervals all during the day.

Rolling, rugged hills, and rocky streams of south Texas slowed our progress. Through a combination of single-minded determination and unspoken resolve, we covered more ground in one day than I could have imagined possible.

My diligent, eagle-eyed partner found the track a few hours into the run, and held to it like an angry badger until the light gave out again. My admiration for Boz and his unsurpassed skill grew with every passing minute. We camped on the banks of a shallow creek off the Rio Hondo that night. Inviting stream inspired me to take a quick bath. Stifling heat of the day gave way to a wonderfully cool evening.

Didn't matter much. Once again, sleep came to me in fits and starts. Every time I closed my tired eyes, Dianna's face appeared on the back of the lids. In some of those visions, she leaned close and whispered, "Changed my mind. Decided I couldn't wait." In others, she called my name and begged me to rescue her from the clutches of men birthed by animals and raised on blood.

At one point, I snapped awake and found myself sitting upright with a pistol in each hand. Boz called out, "You okay over there, Lucius?"

"Sorry. Wasn't my intention to wake you as well."

"You've been talking in your sleep, ole son."

"What'd I say?"

"Well, last thing I heard was, 'Oh, let up on me some. Nothin' I can do right now. Swear I'll take care of it.' Or somethin' to that effect."

"You must've been awake for a spell then."

"Worried 'bout you, ole son. Done said you should try not to let this thing bother you so much. Meant it. We'll arrive in Uvalde by late tomorrow afternoon. Should be able to find out something definite then."

Rolled back into my bedroll. "Certainly hope so. You can't imagine how bad I feel about this whole affair, Boz."

"Given the way you've been actin', think I might have some idea. Trust me, if I can lay hands on anyone who took part in Mrs. Savage's abduction, he'll tell us everything he ever knew — from the day of his birth to a minute before we found him. Way these kinds of bastards run off at the mouth, all we've got to do is hit a few saloons in town, and I'd be willing to bet things start poppin' mighty fast."

True to his word, Boz led us to the outskirts of Uvalde, at a little after three o'clock the following afternoon. We reined up in a stand of live oaks. Leafy, overarching shelter provided respite from an unrelenting sun.

"One of my favorite places in Tejas. Town's widely known for its trees," Boz said as he wiped his neck with a damp bandanna.

Poured water from my canteen over my wrists, took a sip, and ran some down the back of my neck. "They are amazing. Quite beautiful."

"I've heard some even call Uvalde the City of Trees. Feller named Black laid the place out right after the Big Fight. Built a series of plazas all through town. Started out being a right peaceful place to settle. Unfortunately for the clod kickers, these days more'n a few cattle rustlers, horse thieves, pistol fighters, and murderous desperadoes call the town home."

"Coffin must be the worst of 'em."

"They's two bad 'uns down here — John King Fisher and Nate Coffin. Be a right serious job of head scratchin' to figure out which one's the dead-level worst."

"Appears the trail of them that took Dianna leads straight into town, 'less we've missed the mark."

"Yep. Why don't we mosey on in and rattle some cages?"

"Smoky Tiner mentioned a place called Los Lobos. Find it, we'll probably find him."

"Hell, I know that low-life, cow-country oasis. We'll ride right up to it."

"What's your thinkin' on this deal, Boz? Should we go in as Rangers, or remove these badges and sneak in on the sly?"

He threw his head back and chuckled. "Just be damned if I'll take my badge off. Want each and every badman in town to know the Texas Rangers have arrived, that we're mad as hell and on the prod, and that their lives ain't worth a bucket of cold snake piss if they cross us."

"Glad to hear that, Boz. Far as I'm concerned, any man who'd steal a woman for sale into the life of a Mexican whore don't need to live any longer than it'll take to burn the gunpowder to kill 'im." Urged Grizz forward, and over my shoulder added, "And any of them as would help in the effort ain't no better."

Followed the dusty Main Street west through town. Pulled up at the first plaza we reached. Tied our animals on the northeast corner in front of a sizable building project. Sign out front informed those as could read that the city planned on a brand-new opera house once all the hammering, sawing, and such got done.

We pulled shotguns and bandoliers of shells before heading across a tree-shaded square decorated with multicolored streamers, huge batches of bright red hanging chili peppers, and piñatas shaped like a variety of animals.

Every ten or fifteen feet, a smiling, sarape-wearing peon stood behind a rough-wheeled cart set up to sell tacos, tamales, spicy smoked meat on a stick, or sweets. Overwhelming smell of cooked goods permeated the dense, smoke-filled air, and caused my empty stomach to rumble.

"Must be havin' some sort of celebration." I said.

Boz let out a derisive snort. "Mexicans always celebratin' somethin'. Ain't seen one of 'em yet wouldn't do damned near anything for the least excuse to have a party."

We strolled around a fountain where a number of the food sellers, and their customers, suspiciously eyeballed our arrival. Kids and dogs skittered away as we heeled it toward the Los Lobos Cantina and Saloon.

Drew up in the street out front of the rough-looking watering hole, and checked the loads in our big blasters. Then, Boz gave the hooves on several of the horses tied to hitching posts a good going-over.

He slapped the last one on the rump, nodded, and said, "Whoever rode these animals are the ones we want. Paint horse has missing nails in its right rear shoe. Been seein' it on the trail all the way here."

"Well, my good friend, let's step inside and see if we can't stir this wasp's nest up a little. Rattle some cages. Get some attention."

"Anyone goes for a gun, Lucius, don't hesitate. Put 'em down quick, and don't bother tryin' to spare whoever might get in the way. Four barrels of buckshot should take care of damned near anything we find in this scorpion's nest."

"You needn't worry yourself about me, my friend. Anyone makes a move, it'll be his last."

We pushed through the scruffy cantina's batwings shoulder to shoulder. Felt like walking into a cave full of rattlesnakes. Grinning Death eased in behind us and took a place at my elbow.

12

"FOR GOD'S SAKE! DON'T SHOOT NO MORE."

Magnified by an oppressive afternoon's withering heat, the heavy odors of spilt liquor, sweat, vomit, and burning tobacco rolled over us in an odiferous wave that sought an easy outlet through the watering hole's still-swinging doors.

Music, laughter, and general gaiety we'd heard from the street evaporated like spit on a red-hot stove lid. Pair of guitar pickers and a tambourine shaker, in a back corner, had access to a side door, and vanished as sure as fog in the sunshine. Nervous group of local tipplers, who appeared desperate for an exit, carefully pushed each other past me and Boz on their way out the front.

For several seconds, everyone still inside froze in place like animals trapped by a larger and more deadly predator. General merriment and former sense of drunken celebration quickly gave way to instant, air-thickening tension. You'd of thought they surely spied black-robed Death himself, and realized He had accompanied us inside with the intent of sizing up every man with a drink in his hand for a narrow hole in the ground.

Glanced over at the rough-cut, single-plank serving bar that rested on several wooden barrels and ran along most of the right side of an oblong room, about twenty feet across and thirty feet deep. Variety of colorfully labeled bottles, filled with amber and clear liquids, sat on a second plank-and-barrel affair used as the back bar.

Large mirror with a ragged crack, which slashed its way from corner to corner, covered part of the never-been-painted, water-stained wall behind the store of liquor supplies. Wall decorations consisted of Mexican vaquero trappings — hats, spurs, whips, and such — that hung from various nails and wooden pegs around the coarse, dirt-floored liquor emporium.

Skinny, humpbacked, hatchet-faced drink slinger threw a nasty towel over his shoulder. Studied his newest patrons like he'd found a big ole dog deposit in the middle of his floor.

Barely heard him mutter, "Help you gents?" Then he reconsidered, and gingerly backed into the farthest corner away from us and whatever action might be about to occur.

Half a dozen hard-eyed pistoleros loafed at tables arranged in a row on our left that started at the front of the room and headed to the back, where the itinerant band had been set up.

Boz whispered, "You take the first table and the feller against the wall at the middle one. I'll take the back table and the gunny out front at the middle one."

Barely breathed, "Gotcha," as we moved one final step closer to the primary objects of our sharply focused attention.

All the gunmen appeared to have been cut from the same piece of coarse cloth. Dressed in rough canvas pants, covered with weathered leather chaps, most sported short-tailed, open, waist-length Mexican jackets. All wore faded cotton shirts beneath. Each man had a wide-brimmed sombrero pushed back on his shoulders and held in place by a leather thong. Except for a garish variety of still-bright colors in their choice of bandannas, a casual observer would have found himself hard pressed not to describe the bunch as looking like a pack of evil brothers.

Pair of scraggly-haired, snaggle-toothed women, in bosom-revealing party dresses that'd seen better days, scurried for the corner behind the bar and cowered in a spot of safety with their surly employer.

Feller who sported a deep, bone-white scar that ran from his hatband to his stubble-covered chin sat facing us at the middle table, and pitched poker chips into a building pot. With an air of practiced disgust, he laid a fistful of well-used pasteboards aside. Then, he plucked a smoldering, hand-rolled cigarette from between chapped lips, and assumed the manner of one bored all to hell and gone.

He flipped the smoking butt our direction. As it rolled against the toe of Boz's boot, Scar Face sneered, "What you stinkin' gringo law bring-gairs want in heer? Thees a private fandango. You *sabe, es stupidos.*"

Boz ignored the wiseacre; didn't hesitate for a second. "We want all the men who rode in on the horses out front."

"And the *americana* you boys took from a Willow Junction hotel, against her will, a few days back. We're prepared to kill every one you sons of bitches to get her back," I added.

Hombre at the farthest table cast a sneaky glance our direction. One eye was covered with a greasy, crusted, black leather patch, and he sported a gold tooth the size of my thumb in front of a wickedly grinning mouth. "You *pendejos* know where you are? Thees place, thees town, thees whole part of Tejas belongs to his eminence Señor Nate Coffin. We can keel you both like *cucarachas.* No harm weel come to us. You *sabe, mis amigos?*" Then, he grinned at the man across the table and, under his breath, said something that sounded kind of like *"hijos de putas."*

Boz brought his shotgun to bear on the big talker and said, "Boys, you're not talkin' to a pair of no-authority town lawdogs. You're talkin' to the great State of Texas in the persons of Rangers Randall Bozworth Tatum and Lucius 'By God' Dodge. Followed a group of woman-stealin' sons of bitches right to the tables where you're sittin'. Want the lady back. Give 'er up, or die in your chairs."

Gringo rider, decked out in various remnants of a Yankee cavalry uniform, and who sat at the table nearest me, chimed in. "The hell with the great State of Texas and all the badge-totin' sons of Confederates like you in it. Best take your search elsewhere, Rangers." He spit the word "Rangers" out like he'd somehow got a chunk of horse flop in his mouth. "Don't let them batwings hit you boys in yer slow-movin' dumb asses on the way back to the street."

A wave of uneasy laughter rolled from table to table at the poorly thought-out gibe. The bartender and his cadre of fallen women ducked down to the point where all I could see was their wide, unblinking eyes over the edge of the bar.

Bold son of a bitch closest to the wall, at the center table, opened the ball. Didn't recognize him till he raised his head and I could see beneath the brim of his enormous palm-leaf sombrero. Smoky Tiner turned out to be one of those fellers who just couldn't buy a break.

Stupid bastard popped up like a branded bullfrog, kicked his chair aside, and then went for a big Remington pistol tucked behind a red sash around his skinny waist.

Yelped, "By God I kilt ole Pinky Jiles, and now Ranger Lucius Dodge is mine, boys."

Whipped that Remington from under his sarape and fired a thunderous shot that came near on to taking my head clean off. Thumb-sized piece of burning hot lead singed the collar of my shirt and knocked a chunk of splintered wood out of the door frame around the batwings. Any man with half a brain should know it's a hell of a bad move to miss a man pointing a shotgun your direction.

Bet from where I stood there was no more than twelve or fifteen feet between us. Can't till this very instant imagine how ole Smoky managed not to put one in my brain box. Have to credit God with glancing my way that fateful day.

Dropped the hammer on one barrel of buckshot that hit the stupid son of a bitch like a clenched fist. Concussion from the blast sent everyone scurrying for safety. Pressed their noses into the dirt, spittle, and puke decorating the saloon's filthy floor. Tightly bunched wad of shot knocked Tiner backward. Splattered gouts of blood, bone, and bits of clothing all over a three-foot-round chunk in the wall.

Spent black powder spooled across the room in a dense cloud, and almost hid my view of the slow-moving lowlife as he slid to the floor in a growing pool of his own gore. Mouthy murderer's broken corpse rolled under the table and flopped like a chicken that'd just had its neck wrung for Sunday supper. Flying blood and mess from his loosened bowels sprayed everything that couldn't move or get out of the way.

'Bout a dozen pieces of stray lead had peppered both the evil skunks sitting at the front table before they could dive out of the muzzle blast's path. Went to howling like whipped dogs. Hopped up and started slapping at spots in their clothing that sent out wispy strands of gray smoke, along with minor spurts of bright red blood here and there.

Through the bluish-gray fog I'd put into the dense overheated air, Mr. Eye Patch, trembling hands held high over his head, yelped, *"Por Dios!* No shoot no more. No need for thees, Rangers. No one ees drawing on you hombres. *Es mi promesa, amigos."*

We forced all them polecats left alive against the back wall. Boz provided cover while I did everything possible to disarm the snaky crew of kidnappers and killers. Took near twenty weapons off five men, not including all the knives.

One runty little gringo feller had six Colt pistols and one of those big ole French Le Mats on him. That's a hell of a heavy load to tote around. Man packed so much death-dealing iron, it's a wonder he didn't have debilitating back problems, or at least a case of painful kidney stones.

Pitched his last shooter aside and said, "Damn. Can't even begin to imagine how a squirt like you manages to stand upright and walk with a load like this."

He sneered, "Gimme my guns back and

I'll show you Ranger scum just how tough a man I really am, by God."

Made him madder when I grinned real big and said, "Not today. Maybe another time."

Finally got the whole crew against the wall and facing us again. Boz waved his weapon back and forth, and snapped, "Little gunfire and death don't change nothing. Still need an answer to the same question. Where's the woman you boys brought to town?"

Couldn't help but chime in, "And unless you want to end up like the leaky Mr. Tiner over there, somebody had best get to talkin' and right damned quick."

Second or so passed with no response. Breeched my shotgun, pulled out the spent shell casing, and pitched it toward Eye Patch. Big piece of brass rolled across the floor till it hit the heel of his boot and clinked off the rowel of a silver spur.

Replaced the exhausted round with a fresh load. Snapped the weapon shut, cocked both hammers, and brought the muzzle up. Pointed the sawed-off weapon at a bone-thin wretch in the middle of the line. He flashed a mouthful of tobacco-rotted teeth from a grinning, pockmarked face that resembled the surface of a full moon in October.

Ugly wretch went to hopping from foot to foot. Yelped, "D-d-don't get all t-t-twitchy-fingered on me there, Ranger. Ain't no call to shoot. Swear 'fore Jesus, I'll tell you whatever you want."

From the corner of his mouth, Eye Patch muttered, "*Cerra la boca,* Harkey."

Got to give ole ugly-mouthed Harkey credit. He didn't let what was said intimidate him much. "You go to hell, Martinez. You wanna die, go right on ahead. Lead on. Sure these fellers will help you along the way to a handshaking acquaintance with Satan and eternal damnation. Just like they done for Smoky yonder. Think I'll stick around the livin' a bit longer."

Boz bored in on the talker. "Here's your chance for a little in the way of redemption, Harkey. For the third and last time, where's the woman?"

"Ain't for certain sure, and that's the God's truth, Ranger. No one here could testify to her present location with any real confidence. We turned the lady over to Nate Coffin. Right in this very spot. Ain't a man here that don't know that."

I took an angry step his direction and snapped, "Had she come to any harm from you or your sorry compadres' efforts?"

"Not from me, and not as I could see.

Coffin made it crystal clear when he sent us out that he wanted the woman totally unharmed. In pristine condition, as it were. Leastways, that's what he said, pristine. Ain't exactly sure what 'at 'ere word means."

"Where is she now?" Boz asked.

"Nate told us as how he was a-takin' her down to his ranch between here and Carrizo Springs. Had mentioned in the past as how he figured to use her for a spell, and then send her across the border. His place ain't that far from here. Just head south a bit over twenty miles. Cain't miss the turn to the east. Got a sign right out on the road. It's called Rancho Paraíso. Toward the Nueces. Take you there, if'n you want."

Martinez's English cleared up considerable when he turned to our informant and very distinctly said, "Your life ain't worth a bag of week-old Oklahoma chicken shit, Harkey." Came to me that the man's show of broken Mexican speaking was just that — show.

Boz motioned for Harkey to step out. Snaggle-toothed outlaw appeared much relieved. "Won't regret it, fellers. Swear you won't regret it," he said as he hustled over and took a spot behind us.

"What are we gonna do with the rest of 'em, Boz?"

"Townhall Plaza is the next one up the street. Got a serviceable jail there, if memory serves. We'll lock 'em up. Maybe come back and get 'em later. Maybe just leave 'em there to rot."

Harkey coughed and kind of waved like he wanted Boz's attention. "Nate Coffin owns everything around these parts, Ranger. Includin' Marshal Barton Pitt. You lock these here fellers up in Pitt's jail, they won't be there when you come back five minutes later. Probably be out lookin' to kill you boys."

"Don't like to admit it, but he's got a point, Boz," I said.

Tatum shook his head and gazed at the floor for a second. Then, he snapped a glance my way and said, "Main reason for keeping these snakes alive would be the open charges in Salt Valley concerning the murder of Deputy Jiles. But the very dead feller under the table yonder just confessed to that 'un. Guess we'll just have to kill 'em where they stand."

Gunny dressed in the Yankee cavalry duds flinched like he'd been slapped in the face with a dead skunk. "Now, wait just a damned minute here. You cain't just go and execute us like unarmed dogs. By God, that ain't nowhere close to bein' lawful, right, or proper."

Boz threw his head back and let out a devilish cackle that made my skin crawl. Then, he nailed all those no-accounts to the wall with a fierce stare. "As of this instant, I'm all the law you boys might ever get a chance to see in this part of Texas — arresting officer, judge, jury, and executioner. And given the reasons behind us havin' this conversation in the first place, killin' you fellers would seem the easiest solution to a real prickly problem."

Former soldier must have had some lawyer in him. Said, "What if we promise to ride like hell out of Uvalde. Not come back. Get as far away from here as possible. Swear 'fore Jesus you let me go, I'll never come back this way long as I live."

Almost in unison Scar Face, Eye Patch, and the other one said, "*Sí, senor.* Leave plenty pronto. No come back."

Boz glanced my direction again. I shrugged. "Still think it best that we lock 'em up. Wouldn't trust anything this bunch promises. If Marshal Pitt turns 'em out, we'll just lock him up in his own jail. Besides, it's gonna make one helluva mess if we kill 'em all here."

"Well, then, that decides it," Boz said. "You bastards keep your hands in the air.

Get to hoofin' it for the *juzgado*. Any treachery, and I will kill all of you."

Harkey might have been a skunk, but he knew the local marshal for what he was. We left our newly found informant sitting on the boardwalk outside the jail. Boz shook a finger in Harkey's face and said, "Don't you rabbit on me. Swear to God, I'll run you to ground and make you wish your mother never delivered you into this life."

Harkey got all wounded, hurt, and indignant. "Jesus, Ranger. My momma didn't raise no broke-brained idiots. Swear I'll be waitin' right here like a milk-raised hound dog when you come back out."

A barrel-bellied Barton Pitt met us and our angry gang of captives inside the door of his lockup. He immediately went into long-winded and strenuous objections at Coffin's men being incarcerated in his wretched hoosegow.

Once the jumpy star wearer realized we intended to force the issue over his heated protests, he held his hands out and waved at us like a troubled old maid. "Cain't do 'er, gents. Cain't let you house these fellers in my jail. Hell, might as well cut my own throat, right here, right now. You're bound to be aware of the precarious nature of my position. What with Nate Coffin bein' so close and all."

Boz ended the conversation when he laid his shotgun on the trembling man's shoulder and said, "Hand me the key, you useless gob of guts, and get the hell out of my way."

Poor marshal got a horror-stricken look on his ruddy, swollen face like he'd just been confronted by the very real possibility of his own mortality. "Jesus Christ, Rangers, please," he whined.

As we pushed our prisoners past him, and into his empty cells, he moaned, "Coffin *will* find out about this. He'll come blowin' into town, kill me deader than a rotten fence post, and turn all these men loose 'fore the sun goes down."

Paperbacked, and full of bright-yellow mustard, the lawman's cowardly attitude hit me the exact wrong way. Had heard a similar bellyaching complaint in Willow Junction. "Good God Almighty," I shot back. "Ain't no wonder blood letters and badmen run rampant in west Texas. Everyone wearin' a badge out this way is as scared as a jackrabbit in a coyote's hip pocket. Enough to make real men sick to our stomachs."

Boz slammed the last iron-barred cell door closed, and turned the key with a resounding and authoritative metallic click. Swung around on Pitt and threw the keys back at him. "Don't be worryin' about Coffin, Marshal. You've got a much closer and more immediate concern. If I come back here and these men have somehow managed to escape, or got sprung by friends, or called to Heaven by golden-winged angelic messengers fresh from the throne of the living God, you'll have to answer to me."

Just to put some final emphasis on the point, I slapped the agitated lawman on the back and added, "Best do what the man says, Mr. Pitt. Nate Coffin is so sweet he'd cause a cavity in an elephant's tusk compared to Boz Tatum." Pitt threw me back the look of a man about to have a killer stroke.

Out on the boardwalk, Harkey hopped up and grinned like an escaped lunatic. "You fellers all ready to go?"

Boz shouldered his shotgun, scratched his chin, and looked thoughtful. He pulled me away from the cooperative outlaw and almost whispered, "Let's gather our animals up, Lucius. But before we head for the Coffin stronghold, think it best we enlist a bit of death-dealing assistance."

"Death-dealing assistance? What have you got in mind, Boz?"

"Old and dear friend of mine lives a piece west of town. He could well be the decidin' factor in any action we take."

"Wouldn't mind havin' another gun along for the ride, that's for certain sure."

"Not to put too fine an edge on the situation, Lucius, but the truth is I don't necessarily have what you could call anything like complete trust in this snake Harkey. One or the other of us will probably have to keep an eye on him, lest he double-cross us right into an early grave."

"Don't worry, Boz," I said, "I'll watch him."

We started back toward the cantina to pick up our animals, and motioned for Harkey to follow. I slapped Boz on the back and said, "Is there any part of Texas where you don't have friends?"

"Not as I'm aware of. My dear ole white-haired, sainted pappy always told me as how it pays not to burn your bridges behind you as you ride through the difficult trials and tribulations of this life. Thus far, that ill-educated horse raiser has proven out as absolutely correct. Nothing to match havin' friends you can call on in times of dire need. Right now, we require the assistance of a big gun. And I just happen to know where to find the biggest of 'em all, retired Ranger

Ox Turnbow."

"Jesus, Boz, you know the one and only Ox Turnbow?"

"Not only do I know him, but the old bandit owes me big-time. And if memory serves, he's less than ten miles from where we're standin' right this minute."

13

"GUNSMOKE AND BLOOD, BY GOD . . ."

We pointed our animals north and west toward the Nueces River. Harkey trailed behind like a whipped dog. Maybe five miles out of town, Boz turned us back south, along a narrow track that led into the rough-and-tumble of low mesquite-littered bluffs, grass-covered hills, and rocky ravines.

Hadn't gone all that far when we came on a rude wooden sign with lettering burned into it with a hot running iron. Rough marker warned wayward travelers that YORE ON OX TURNBOW'S LAND — GO BACK OR GIT KILT DEAD.

Pointed message got my undivided attention. Said, "Reckon your former amigo would shoot us, Boz?"

"Could easily happen. Ox always has been just about two shades meaner'n horned Satan hisself. But I doubt he'd plug an old compadre." He thought on my question a second or so longer, and then added, "Just to be on the safe side of the question, we'll tie us a piece of white rag to our rifle barrels. Hold 'em skyward, butts against our saddles. Don't think he'd shoot anyone under a white flag. Hope not leastways."

Harsh path eventually narrowed down between scrub-infested, steep-walled bluffs to a point where the trail got tight for any more than two animals to pass abreast. Sheer, natural barriers on either side quickly added to the cramped and uncomfortable feelings that already plagued my overactive and fevered mind.

Boz led the way, and reined up of a sudden. Couldn't see around him to what had hindered our progress. But then I heard him say, "Damnation, Ox. You wouldn't go and plug an old friend, now would you?"

A voice, some distance ahead, that sounded like a rusted crosscut saw going through a rotten tree, called out, "Well, kiss my saddle-calloused, leathery old ass. If it ain't the real, live, and original Randall Bozworth Tatum, I'll eat a week-dead armadiller. Come on in, you ugly son of a bitch."

He must have motioned for us to follow. Boz waved me and Harkey ahead. As we moved forward, the course finally opened out on a sweeping, treeless vista that appeared to run onto the ends of the earth —

or at least that part of west Texas a bit before you get to the Rio Grande and the wilds of northern Mexico.

Our slow-moving party passed grazing cattle, horses, and a number of well-kept outlying corrals. Greeted by a pack of barking dogs, we finally arrived in front of a comfortable-looking combination adobe, slate, and stone house, located within walking distance of a handy creek. Sheltered under the only real trees in sight, Turnbow's rugged homestead was, beyond doubt, the solitary residence for at least twenty miles in any given direction. Lonely site finalized my impression that the man loved his privacy.

Mounted into the side of a low, south-facing hill, the isolated ranch's central building looked to have been painstakingly constructed almost exclusively from materials found cropping up from the unforgiving soil all around the semiarid location. Feller leading us reined up out front, and stepped down from a long-legged blood bay mare.

All I can say on the subject of his appearance is that Ox Turnbow looked absolutely nothing like his brutish moniker would lead a reasonable, thinking man to believe he might. Maybe five foot seven or eight, lean as a chewed leather thong, and weathered to the color of aged copper, he waved us off our animals, grabbed Boz soon as he could, and hugged him like a long-lost brother.

Famed gunman pushed away, slapped Boz's shoulder, and said, "Just be damned. If they's one man I never expected to see in these wild and woolly parts, it'd have to be you, old friend. Figure they's gotta be a reason, though. Dangerous man killer like you didn't just show up on my doorstep by accident, did you, Tatum?"

Boz smiled and said, "Always get right to the point, don't you, Ox?"

Wiry rancher showed a mouthful of pearly whites and shook his head. "No need to go a-beatin' 'round the bush, is they? Life's way too short, don't you think?"

Our urgent reason for being in such a remote location got put to the side just a bit longer when Boz turned and motioned my direction. "This here's my Ranger partner, Lucius Dodge, Ox. Want you two to shake hands, and be good friends."

Legendary former Ranger removed a skintight, leather glove and extended a work-roughened hand that jutted from a fringed shirt. Grip like iron bands surrounded my fingers and, right nigh, turned my knuckles into dust. My discomfort caused a subtle, toothy grin that crinkled the skin at the corner of chapped lips set in his weather-bronzed face.

"Most pleased to make your acquaintance, Lucius Dodge. Any friend of this old bandit is damned sure a friend of mine. Wasn't for Tatum here, I'd of been dead at least a dozen times. Man saved me from a sulfurous hell, and eternity carryin' a pitchfork, on more occasions than I care to remember."

Boz toed the dirt and got all humble. Snatched his hat off and slapped it against his leg. "Well, now, I'd have to declare as how we've likely worked out about even in the life-saving business. But you do owe me a big'un for that time over in Cuero. Remember that little dustup?"

Turnbow ducked his head for a second. His weather-scarred hand darted to Boz's shoulder. "Won't never forget Cuero, Boz. Never. Weren't for you, Felthus Boggs mighta blowed my head clean off. Why don't you boys turn your animals out in the corral and come on inside? Personally guarantee it's much cooler. We'll have a snort and recall old times."

Boz put Harkey to taking care of our animals. Squirrelly little thug liked doing chores not one little bit, but wasn't allowed no hell of a lot of choice in the matter.

We stepped inside Turnbow's stone house

to discover a single, high-ceilinged room made possible by a dirt floor dug out to a bit over two feet below ground level. The central room, the largest open area, was arranged around a fireplace fully capable of roasting an entire steer. Individual corners served as concealable sleeping and dining areas. All the walls and posts sported decorations that ranged from animal skulls to every kind of firearm imaginable.

Amazed, Boz said, "Damn, but you were right, Ox. It is one helluva lot cooler in here. Wouldn't have believed it from what I seen outside."

Could easily spot the old Ranger's pride in his home as it danced in his steel-gray eyes. He grinned and waved around the room. "Dug in and built 'er tighter'n the bark on a bois d'arc tree. She's cool in the summer and right toasty in the winter. Cain't beat it for comfort or security."

"Mighty fine," I said.

"You boys take a seat there at the table. Built it myself. Chairs made mostly out of horns I found out in the brush, or bobbed off'n meaner members of my own herds. Cushions is skins off'n deer, antelope, and buffeler what I kilt over the years. Brought all the cut lumber you can see out from the only sawmill in Uvalde. Took me near five years to finish this place."

Boz said, "Thought you had a woman, Ox. Mexican gal named Lolita, if memory serves."

Turnbow shook his head and stared at the floor. "Yeah, well, she passed two years back. Died in childbirth."

Could see he'd stepped into a painful area, so Boz said, "Sorry to hear that, old friend. Know you came out this way and built your place with her in mind."

Our host threw his hat into an empty chair and shrugged. "Know how it is, Boz. Life's mighty cheap out here in the big cold and lonely. 'Specially hard on womenfolk."

He rummaged in a glass-fronted cabinet on one side of the fireplace and returned with a nice-sized corked jug. Dropped the heavy container on the table with a resounding thump, and flopped into the skin-covered chair beside me. Soon, tin cups brimmed with powerful, tongue-scorching home brew.

On the second pass at Turnbow's bonded-in-the-barn brand of tarantula juice, Boz moved the conversation away from Lolita Turnbow's untimely departure and got us down to the deadly business behind our visit.

With his half-empty cup, my amigo

pointed to a massive weapon hanging over the mantelpiece. "See you've still got that big, ole beast killer of a rifle, Ox."

Turnbow threw his hat on the table. "The Sharps? Hell, yes, I've still got 'er. Never give Matilda up. When the goin' got tough, that ole gal saved my bacon, more times than I care to think on, from starvation, poverty, and bloodthirsty Injuns."

Boz took another sip of liquid fire, leaned across the table, and looked deadly serious. "You still hit a gnat's ass from a quarter mile away with 'er?"

Turnbow scratched a stubble-covered chin, wagged his head from side to side, then said, "Figured if I got a bit of ole tangle-leg down your gullet, Tatum, the reason for this uncommon visit would finally come out. What you got in mind, amigo?"

"Would have told you without the lubricating effects of anything like this here gut-warmin' batch of homemade espiritus fermenti, pard. But today you're right on target. This ain't no tea-cake-and-doily social call. Tell our friend why we're here, Lucius."

Kept the ugly tale as brief as I could. Tried to get all the essentials in. Did dwell, a bit, on the parts about the uncalled-for death of

Dianna's innocent young son and how she'd been taken. Turnbow appeared to get more agitated with each and every lawless revelation. Appeared to me as though the abuse of women, in any form or manner, had the power to really light a fire under the man.

Eventually he held a hand up as though to stop me. Shook his head in disgust and said, "Hell, boys, I've been lookin' for an excuse to rid the world of that lawless bastard's shadow for years. When first I moved to these parts, Coffin and some of his crew tried to run me off. Took more'n a head or two of my stock over the years, and he's murdered some of my men in the past. Kilt a few of his'n in return, though. Put out word as how if anything else wayward happened on my spread again, or to any of my vaqueros, I'd be after him personal."

"Must've had the desired effect," I said.

"Well, Lucius, ain't had no trouble with Nate since. Nowadays, him and his boys take heed to the sign you seen on your way in. All of 'em know beyond any doubt I will kill 'em deader'n hell on an outhouse door if they even so much as show their ugly faces around my spread."

Boz sounded amused when he said, "Just knowin' you're here keeps 'em away?"

"Well, yeah. And the fact that I done

215

already went and pulled almost half a dozen of 'em up by the roots over the years. Sons of bitches are fully aware they'd best not be pesterin' me or mine. Matilda'll come down from her perch and Coffin men'll start dyin' 'fore they even know what hit 'em. All they'll hear is a whistling buzz and, 'fore they can spit, Jesus'll be sayin' howdy."

Suppose my friends could hear the emotion in my voice when I got down to brass tacks and said, "We ain't got much time to debate this, fellers. Gotta come up with a workable plan real quick — tonight if at all possible. Longer we dally, the more chance for Coffin to do what he's threatened and send Dianna farther south."

"Harkey allows as how he can find Nate's stronghold. Says he'll lead us there," Boz added.

Turnbow took a heavy dollop from his cup. Wiped away the residue on the sleeve of his shirt. "No real problem findin' Coffin. Don't need no half-assed badman like Harkey for that."

Surprised me a bit. "That a fact?"

"Ain't foolin' with you, Lucius. Anyone with the grit can just head south and east of here, about forty mile, and turn for the Nueces. Coffin's snake den is damned near exactly midway between Uvalde and Carrizo Springs, hard by the river. No fences, no walls. Cain't miss 'im 'less you're blinder'n a snubbin' post. Ain't no fortress or nothin'."

"Now that's a surprise," I offered. "Figured on a fortified stronghold of some kind. Thought sure we'd end up using dynamite to get inside."

"Oh, hell, no. Nothing like that. The wall around Coffin's place is nothin' more'n a determined force of armed and vicious men. He usually has twenty or more hired killers about. Hell, anybody with nerve enough can ride right up to the front porch and say howdy. 'Course that all depends on whether Nate's feelin' charitable, keeps his gun thugs leashed, and lets you live that long."

"You believe they'd go and murder a badge-wearin' Ranger bold enough to ride right up to the front door, Ox?" I asked.

Boz looked anxious and puzzled. "What 'er you gettin' at, Lucius."

"What if I confront Coffin with the absolute error of his wicked ways. Propose that he turn Dianna over to me, or die if he don't. If Ox is as good with that Sharps as you've both led me to believe, you boys could hide somewhere nearby, cover me when I ride in, and kill anyone who gets feisty during the negotiations."

Boz gave his head a determined shake. "Don't care for such hastily thought-out plans one little bit, Lucius. Far as I'm concerned, you goin' in alone is way too dangerous a prospect to consider."

"Now, wait a minute, Tatum." Turnbow stood, moved to his mantel, and lifted the heavy Sharps from its deer-horn cradles. He turned, made his way back to the still-warm chair, resumed his seat, and caressed the weapon as though it were a living thing. "The boy just might have a workable idea goin' here, Boz. Could be the ticket, you know."

"What the hell are you sayin', Ox? Damnation, this ain't nothin' like what I had in mind."

Turnbow flipped up the peep sight on the Sharps, shouldered the weapon, and peered down the barrel. "Well, what did you have in mind, *mi amigo bueno?*"

"Well, think the three of us should ride in, kill as many as we can, and take the woman back. Each of us can easily blast hell out of seven of 'em, and the whole party's over — right then and there. Gunsmoke and blood, by God, them's the only things men like Coffin, and those skunks as work for him, understand."

I said, "Far as it goes, Boz, I think you're

right. And given any other time and place, I'd be by your side blazin' away in such an endeavor. But if Dianna Savage is still present at Coffin's stronghold, those who took the girl might kill her before we can get in and do anything by way of savin' her. Don't know as how I could live with such an unacceptable outcome."

Turnbow breeched the massive weapon in his lap, examined the action with a cocked eye, and said, "If nothin' else, they's one thing we gotta do immediatelike."

Pulled tobacco and makin's from my shirt pocket. "What would that be?"

Ox snapped, "Git rid of that stink sprayer, Harkey. We don't need 'im. The man's a liability in the best of circumstances and could very well be a spy."

"But he has to show us the way," Boz offered.

"Hell, everyone around these parts knows how to get to Nate Coffin's place. I could find that rat's nest in my sleep. Trust me, fellers, we don't have any need of Harkey. And more importantly, he could end up gettin' us kilt if'n we didn't watch his sorry hide every minute. I don't trust back-shootin', scurvy little curs like Harkey any farther than I can throw an anvil. We gotta git shed of him right now. Cain't wait."

Boz grudgingly took the responsibility of telling Harkey to hit the trail running. Man didn't like the way things turned out in the least. Wanted to argue the point for a spell. I soon got the impression Turnbow had rightly spotted something in him neither Boz nor I had figured on.

Eventually the old Ranger stepped into the rising fracas himself. He waved the Sharps in the nervy outlaw's face and told him how the cow ate the cabbage. Agitated bandit fogged out pretty quick, once he knew his life might actually be in some serious jeopardy again.

Guess he'd just about got completely out of sight when Ox said, "Damn. Now as I think on it, fellers, mighta been best to have kilt the belly-slinkin' snake. Bet he runs straight to Coffin."

"Let 'im," I said.

"Why so?"

"Probably just as well word gets around as how there's angry Rangers about and what they're doin' in these parts. Coffin should have already heard somethin', bein' as we done went and locked up a number of his boys over in Uvalde. If ole Nate knows we're comin', maybe he'll think twice about doin' anything real stupid. Man has to know that if he or his kills either or both of us, the whole of west Texas will be knee-deep in red-eyed Rangers faster'n a hummingbird's heartbeat."

Boz said, "You're right, Lucius, but I'm with Ox on this 'un. Think we probably shoulda killed Harkey."

Went back to our cups, decided on the plan pert near the way I'd outlined it. Ox said, "They's a little tree-shaded hill 'bout five hundred yards from Coffin's front porch. Ideal spot to hide our animals and get the Sharps unlimbered. With Boz spottin' for me, I can easily kill anything what moves. Hell, I can do it without him spottin' for me. Kilt many a buffalo alone. Men is just as easy to dispatch as big dumb animals when they ain't expectin' it."

Boz allowed as how he'd think the whole deal over. "Might be best if I go in with you, Lucius. That way Ox can provide more'n enough cover. Two of us Rangers showin' up should give Coffin a more formidable problem to ruminate about."

Around daylight the next morning, we had everything pretty much decided, and were loaded and ready for a fight. Stuck around long enough for Turnbow's head vaquero to show and get instructions for the stretch *el jefe* would be gone. Headed out for Coffin's Nueces River stronghold just about the time the sun got up good.

As we rode south, my heaving mind filled itself with how I'd respond upon first confronting the son of a bitch responsible for taking Dianna. Knew it would require all my hard-learned self-control to keep from killing the scurvy bastard the instant we met. But Dianna's life could well be at stake, and my only recourse involved an iron-willed effort to stay cool as a skunk in the moonlight no matter what might occur — even discovery of the worst outcome imaginable.

Truth always has been, though, you just never know what might happen when armed and angry men confront each other. Sun-bleached afternoon quickly headed toward the hotter-than-hell-under-an-iron-skillet level. I shuddered like a man freezing to death as I let myself dwell too long on deadly possibilities.

14

". . . YOU'RE GONNA SUFFER THE TORTURES OF THE DAMNED . . ."

"Seems awful quiet for an outlaw headquarters, don't it, boys?" I scanned Nate Coffin's ranch house and surrounding landscape through a set of nearly worn-out surplus cavalry binoculars. Couldn't see a living soul outside. "Only four animals in the corral nearest the big house, Boz. Could be a good sign."

Dropped the glasses to my chest. Let them dangle from their chewed-up leather straps. Turned and watched as Boz pulled his hat off. He wiped sweat from a drenched brow with a faded blue neckerchief. Mopped out the inside of the battered head cover.

"Reckon we done went and got blind lucky for once. You think maybe we mighta caught Coffin at home while his band of henchmen are busy elsewhere, Ox?" he asked.

Turnbow lay on his stomach and stretched his wiry frame out atop a well-used horse blanket. He'd wallowed out a comfortable spot, then worked at refining precise adjustments on Matilda's stock-mounted peep sight. The big Sharps was nestled between a pair of sandbags we'd filled on site a few minutes before.

Old Ranger had set up his ambush nest on the exact same mesquite- and tree-sheltered rise he'd described when we formed our hasty plans for the raid. Not satisfied with the results of his efforts with the gun's adjustable target sight, Ox leaned to the left on his elbow. Squint-eyed, he gazed through a brass-barreled telescope clamped to a short-legged tripod.

"Surely looks to be the case," Ox mumbled, as much to himself as in answer to Tatum's question. "Don't look to be hardly anybody about. Right peaceful."

Former buffalo hunter snorted, turned the knurled knob on the peep a few more clicks, checked the range one more time, and finally nodded his approval. "Any targets are gonna be just under three hundred yards away, boys. Missed my guess on the distance by a mite, but hell, she won't be no problem. Could easily hit a fly sittin' on the hitch rail from this distance with Matilda." He slid a huge brass-jacketed .44–70 shell into the breech and levered it closed.

"One last time. 'Fore we open the ball on this 'un. Just want everyone to be mighty clear on what's about to play out," I said.

"Hell, Lucius, we understand what we're supposed to do," Boz snorted. "Don't we, Ox?"

Turnbow rolled onto one side and rested his head in a cupped hand. He feigned a degree of self-righteous indignation and said, "Damned right. Our mamas didn't raise no egg-suckin' idiots. Me 'n Boz wuz doin' this kinda man killin' 'fore you wuz borned, boy." He struggled to his feet and slapped dust from a leather shirt and breeches.

Boz said, "We once used the same kinda trick on a bunch of the wildest murderin' red savages what ever lived. Killed more'n twenty of 'em. Let me tell you, they were some kind of a mighty surprised party of blood-smeared Ko-manch that death-dealin' afternoon, and that's for damned sure."

"Humor me, fellers," I said. "Here's the drop-dead, final plan. Boz and me ride up to the front door. We move as far to one end of the porch as we can, to give you a good shot, Ox. From here, looks like we'll likely be on your left."

Turnbow smiled and nodded. "If anything

wayward occurs, even something you boys might not see or recognize, I'll drop the first man. Coffin, if possible."

"Right. Then me and Boz'll pull our weapons and finish up. You cover us till it's over and they're all down. Come a-runnin' quick as you can after."

Ox pulled another of the huge cartridges from the belt around his waist and rubbed its lead bullet on his sleeve. "Works for me," he said. "Just hope I get the chance to nail Nate to the wall while we're here. Hell, wouldn't hurt my feelin's none if'n you boys was to just go on ahead and pick a fight so I can send the murderin' cur for his appointed rendezvous with Beelzebub."

Slapped the grip on my belly gun. Said, "That could very well be the way of things, but we want to keep him alive long enough to find out where Dianna is."

Turnbow flashed a toothy grin at the possibility of putting large-caliber holes in Nate Coffin. "Be aware, though," he said. "I'm gonna be firin' at speed. You boys won't hear the muzzle blast right when I start a-shootin'. Gonna be a buzzin' zip in the air. Target'll drop like he's been hit with a Southern Pacific Railroad coal shovel. Count off at least two seconds, and then the report'll finally come. Y'all clear on that 'un?"

Boz stuffed his hat back on a sweaty head. "If I hear anything that even sounds like a zip, I'm gonna blast every living thing in front of my pistols."

Me and Tatum made our way down the far side of the hill to our animals and got mounted. As we moseyed along, checked over our weapons, and nerved up for the coming fight, I said, "Sure you're ready for this one, Boz?"

He nodded and holstered his belly gun. "Damned right, Lucius. I was born ready. Let 'er buck."

Nate Coffin's impressive headquarters presented an appearance that can only be described as totally out of place. Erected in the middle of a Mississippi cotton patch or mossy Louisiana bayou, the grandiose, blindingly white, colonnaded two-story structure would have gone virtually unnoticed. Sitting in the middle of a damned near treeless west Texas plain, between the Rio Grande and the Nueces, the extravagant dwelling had the absolute power to command inquisitive attention from any but the blindest and most indifferent of passersby.

We'd got about halfway to the rambling structure when four men, bristling with rifles and pistols, stepped onto the deep, shaded veranda. Three wore bullet-filled cartridge bandoliers across their chests, pistol belts, and carried Winchester rifles. Appeared they served as protective escorts for a fourth man, who sported a strange-looking vest and strode fearlessly to the front of the rough-looking pack.

Leader of the group hooked his thumbs over a gleaming, concho-embellished pistol rig, threw his chest out, and bulled up in a way that made his authority unmistakable. Couldn't think why, but I got the distinct feeling we had ridden into the presence of a man possessed by moods that could shift with less than a moment's notice.

"Bet you that's the whole of them," Boz said. "Think you were right, Lucius. Rest of Coffin's killers must surely be gone some-wheres."

"Good. Gonna make this raid easier than we ever had any right to expect."

"Just so's there ain't no doubt in your mind, my friend, that's Nate Coffin wearing the leopard-skin vest."

"Leopard skin? Damn, folks got leopards to deal with in these parts?"

"Not as I know of. Rumors have it that a travelin' circus came through these parts some years ago. Way I heard the tale, Nate attended one of their shows. Took an uncommon likin' to their leopard. Tried to buy the beast. When the owner wouldn't sell, Nate shot hell out of the poor feller. Took the cat, kilt it, and had the hide tanned. Hear tell he has a pair of chaps and a hat to match. Wears the whole getup at parties, fandangos, and such. Must be one helluva sight to behold in its total splendiferousness."

"Well, the vicious polecat might be a gaudy dresser on top of all his other less-than-favorable traits, but I'll tell you true, Boz, thought sure he'd be bigger."

"Man's a runt, no doubt about it. If'n he was anywhere close to the size of his reputation, we'd both need one of them Sharps rifles like Turnbow's to bring the bigheaded son of a bitch down."

Life-giving Nueces River ran north and south no more than a quarter of a mile behind Coffin's pretentious dwelling. Numerous irrigation ditches brought water to the main house and, as a consequence, this resulted in the only green spot for many miles in any direction.

We rode through the deep patch of lush, well-kept grass out front of the house, and pulled up at the corner of his porch — according to plan. Followed Boz's lead. Tied my reins to the saddle horn. Tapped Grizz on the neck. He went spraddle-legged, a stance I'd taught him in preparation for deadly action. Placed one hand on my belly gun and the other on my weak-side hip pistol.

Our actions forced all four men away from the doorway of the gaudy hacienda and made them move our direction. Coffin stepped out front and took the lead. Waved his bodyguards to spots on either side and behind him. Hombre to his left hopped down from the porch and, in an obvious flanking move, boldly strode into the yard.

Boz motioned for him to stop. "That's far enough, mister. Get any more to my back side, and I'll be forced to plug you right where you stand."

Coffin threw his head back and laughed. "Guess you'd best pull up right where you are, Mr. Shipman. Wouldn't want anything wayward to happen to you right here in front of my home." Surly gunman grinned like a cat playin' with a mouse, but he stopped and didn't move again.

"You know who we are, Coffin?" I asked.

"Hell, yes, I know who you are, Ranger Dodge. Have more'n twenty men out lookin' for you boys as we speak. Gotta admit, though, you fellers got a lot of hard bark growin' mighty tight on your more'n dumb asses to ride right up to my fancy, straight-from-New-Orleans, leaded-glass front door." He pushed a silver-studded, palm-leaf sombrero off a shaggy-haired noggin and let the wide-brimmed head covering hang against his back on a gold-tipped leather thong.

Couldn't help but notice an ugly scar that sliced down the outlaw chieftain's scalp, ran from the middle of his skull and thence all the way to an eyebrow, split in half by the same jagged white weal. Man had the kind of flat, dead-looking black eyes you'd expect to find on a wild animal in the midst of a bloody kill. Even more unnerving, one of his ears had gone missing. Looked to have been lopped off clean as a whistle.

Figured Coffin's fierce appearance probably proved disconcerting for uninitiated pilgrims and stupid gunhands desperate for a payday. Man stood about five foot six. Stack-heeled, knee-high boots gave him another three inches or so. Just broad enough, and tall enough, to make a good target — no farther than he'd stopped from where I sat.

Tickled the bone grip of my .45 and for a second, actually said a silent prayer that the murderous, woman-stealing piece of walking garbage would do something stupid so I could kill him on the spot. Thought better of such action upon remembering as how I needed the stink-spraying polecat alive — for a little while longer anyway.

Coffin pulled the stump of a dying cheroot from between thin lips, thumped ash off the smoking end, and spit toward my mount's feet. "You law-bringing bastards done already went and killed some of my men. Put some in jail over in Uvalde as well."

"Kidnappers, thieves, and murderers every one," Boz snorted.

"Went and scared Marshal Pitt so bad, that silly, silly man had the unvarnished nerve to get up on his hind legs and tell me he couldn't let my boys go. Wouldn't let 'em go. Felt real bad 'bout killin' 'im, you know. But hell, just couldn't be helped. Cain't have that kind of unthinking disobedience on the part of my hired help. You Rangers do understand, don't you?"

Words that came out of Boz Tatum sounded like icy daggers flung from the black bottom of an open grave. "You killed Barton Pitt 'cause of the responsibility we placed on that poor, all-gurgle-and-no-guts coward."

Coffin glanced at each of the burly gun-men around him. Let out a grating superior-than-thou chuckle. "Why, yes. Yes, I did,

Ranger Tatum," he said, then stuffed the cheroot back in his mouth and threw a big toothy grin Boz's direction.

"Well, I hope you at least gave him a quick send-off," Boz said.

Coffin threw his head back and laughed, then said, "Hanged the fat bastard as a matter of pure fact. Sat on my horse and watched him choke. Took almost ten minutes for the thick-necked stack of horse dung to die. Messed his pants. Helluva stink. Bet fifty dollars he's still a-dangling. Informed Uvalde's upstandin' citizens they'd best leave him swing till I told 'em different. Said I'd burn the whole town to the ground if'n they took him down 'thout my permission. And I'll do it too."

Snapped a quick glance at Boz out of the corner of my eye. Back of my less-than-predictable partner's neck flamed up like something akin to the color of a burning barn in New Hampshire. He'd shifted most of his attention to the gunhand that'd moved off the porch. Knew beyond any doubt the fur was about to fly. Felt the deadly tension in a wave of prickly flesh that ran up my spine, across sweaty shoulders, and down to my fingertips. Gave the whole situation about one more second's thought, and figured there wasn't any need putting the dance off any longer.

Said, "Well, Coffin, guess if you know who we are, you know why we're here."

Toothy grin flickered at the corner of his bluish-purple tobacco-stained lips. "Oh, hell, yes. You boys is lookin' to find 'at 'ere bitch of a whore what went and kilt my younger brother, Reuben."

There's just always been something about the word "bitch" when used to describe any woman I know and respect that has the instant power to send me right over the proverbial edge. Soon as it popped out of Coffin's filthy mouth, his fate was sealed like a Mason jar of my mother's homemade pickles.

That's when I shot him — the first time. Had my favorite bone-gripped Colt out so fast, Coffin didn't even have time to think another evil thought. Nearly fifty years have passed since that moment, and I can still see the flash of shock and surprise in his eyes when I ripped off the round that brought him down.

Big .45 roared, and the heavy slug caught ole Nate about a hand's width below his collarbone. Knocked him three feet. He stumbled backward on wobbly legs. Went down like a felled cottonwood. Knew it wouldn't kill the filthy-mouthed scum, but wanted him on his back — and helpless — while me and Boz dealt with his three henchmen.

Hammer of my pistol had barely dropped on Coffin when Boz put a murderous, thundering shot in the man who'd stepped off the porch. Noise caused Boz's mount to spin around in a tight, terrified circle in a futile, bug-eyed effort at getting away from the violence and death-dealing racket.

Them other two bodyguards never even got an opportunity to raise their arms. Burning zip of hot lead dropped the man nearest the porch rail with a skull shot that splattered blood, brain matter, and bone all over his stunned, horrified cohort. Less than half an eyeblink later, the only gunny left got snatched into the air by Ox Turnbow's invisible hand too. The .44–70 slug smacked the poor sucker in the chest and bounced his shattered, flopping corpse off the wall like a little girl's favorite raggedy doll made from discarded corn shucks.

Hopped off Grizz in the midst of a thick, roiling, bluish-gray haze of spent gunpowder. Boz finally got control of his animal, climbed down, and fired a pair of fatal shots into his still-twitching target.

I jumped onto the porch. Found all Coffin's weapons I could and threw them aside.

Grabbed the bigheaded desperado by the collar. He moaned and whined as I dragged his sorry ass down the steps, and propped him against the fancy iron post that held up the hitch rail.

His head lolled from side to side. He clumsily pawed at the bloody wound in his chest. Fired a wide-eyed, accusatory glance my direction. "You shot me. Damn you. Shot me. Rode right up to my very own house and shot hell out of me — Nate Coffin. Cain't believe it. Ain't supposed to happen like this. I'm the most dangerous and influential man in these parts. Just cain't assassinate a man of my vast importance this a-way."

Refreshed my belly gun and cocked it again. "Yeah, well, your brand of pretentious self-importance don't mean spit to me."

"Damn you Ranger bastards," Coffin wailed. "If'n all my boys was here, you'd both be dead right now."

Boz strolled over and stood beside me. He flipped the loading gate of his pistol open and dumped three spent shell casings at Coffin's feet. Blew into the empty cylinder chambers, reloaded, snapped the gate closed, and recocked the weapon.

"Go ahead, Lucius," Boz said. "Best ask

him now. He don't come up with an answer, I'm gonna do all of west Texas a big favor and kill the son of a bitch deader'n Santa Anna."

"Where's the woman? Where's Dianna Savage?" I snapped. "Tell me now and it'll save you a wagonload of pain, Coffin."

He tried to prop himself up a bit higher on the post, grimaced, and sneered, "Is that a fact? And what're you hymn-singin' pilgrims gonna do if'n I ain't willin' to say one way or 'tother on that particular subject?"

Boz shot him in the foot. Damned near blew the entire sole of his lizard-skin boot off. Couple of his toes flew into the air and landed on his pants leg. Thunderous blast, and a raging case of bloodlust, spurred me to put one in the wounded brigand's other shoulder.

Fast as a good horse could travel, Ox was hoofin' it our direction. Said later he heard Coffin squeal from near two hundred yards away. Swore the man sounded like a panther with a red-hot fire poker up its butt. Coffin yelped and puked a bucketful all over his fancy leopard-skin vest. Wallowed in the pukey dirt for a good two minutes while me and Boz stood by and watched. Swear 'fore Jesus, the man rolled around like a stomped-on rattler.

'Bout the time Ox reined up and hopped down, I bent over Coffin, propped him up again, and said, "Look at me, you woman-stealin' son of a bitch." Those flat, dead, now-bloodshot eyes wobbled around in a sweat-drenched skull as he glared back at me. "This dance could go on for a spell. We've used this particular method of inter-rogation before. Have it refined down to an art. Me and my partner can take as much time as necessary to get what we want out of you."

Boz pulled a second pistol and cocked it. "Damned right. Best get to jackin' them jaws, Nate. Otherwise, in about twenty minutes ain't gonna be much left of either of your legs. Gonna shoot you to itty-bitty pieces, one sorry-assed inch at a time. Get through with them legs, gonna start on your arms."

Coffin's words came out slurred, bloody, and pukey-smelling. "Cain't treat an impor-tant man this a-way. I own every politician, sheriff, and marshal within a hundred miles. You boys is lawmen. Ain't no justice in kill-in' any man like this."

Ox Turnbow stood with the Sharps lying across his arm. Shook his head and said, "Damnation, Nate. Where in the blue-eyed hell does a skunk like you get off thinkin' he's entitled to anything like civilized justice? You've robbed, raped, killed, and plundered all over these parts for more'n twenty years. Know of at least a dozen fine folk you personally put in the ground before the Good Lord even expected them. Time's done arrived to pay up for all your vicious past deeds. We're here to collect."

Ole Nate moaned and tried to roll onto his stomach. I grabbed him by the collar and got him sitting up again. "Never heard of no Rangers what shot a man to bits over the fate of a woman," he said.

Snatched up a handful of his hair and yanked him close. "You've already had your revenge on the lady. Men under your command came to that poor woman's home. Murdered her beautiful, young son. Now you'll tell me where she is or I swear 'fore a benevolent Jesus, you're gonna suffer the tortures of the damned right here on earth. Gonna start the next round of unbelievable pain right here."

Pressed my pistol muzzle against his elbow. Already perforated outlaw made a sound like a pig being slaughtered with a penknife. "Wait, oh, God, please wait," he screeched. "Just give me a second. Please."

Backed away and pulled out my pocket watch. "Gonna give you sixty of 'em. Start-in' right now. No answer to my question *before* your time runs out, and I'll turn your elbow into bloody bone splinters and stringy mush."

"Jesus. Oh, sweet Jesus, save me."

Boz got a chuckle out of the outlaw's entreaty to the Son of God. "Think you mighta waited a bit late to get on a first-name basis with the Lord's Only Begotten Son, Nate. Best get to directin' what energy you've got left to answerin' my compadre's question."

"Alfonso. Alfonso Bejarano."

"Who's Alfonso Bejarano?" I asked.

"Sent the Savage woman to Alfonso."

"Who the hell is he?" Boz yelled.

"Owns a whorehouse down in Nuevo Laredo. La Flor Amarilla."

Blind rage swarmed all over me. Stomped on Coffin's shot-through foot as hard as I could. Heard all them broken bones in his bloody boot crunch and grind. Son of a bitch screamed like a little girl, sat bolt upright, then flopped over, rolled to his side again, and oozed more of his life into the dirt.

Bent down close to his ear, jerked him back up, and snapped, "You did what?"

Have to admit, ole Nate had grit. Man was haughty and stupid, but he did have

240

grit. Turned a snotty nose and gore-dripping mouth right into my face and snarled, "Sent the woman to Bejarano. Figured that'd show her, and anybody related to 'er, just how dangerous it is to mess with any member of the Coffin family."

He'd said more than enough, but just couldn't keep his filthy mouth shut. Still don't know to this very second why he felt it necessary to add, "Even if she's still alive, Dodge, woman ain't never gonna forget us Coffins. Them Messicans'll ride that murderin' slut like a kid's go-round at a travelin' carnival."

Well, that ripped the rag off the bush, for sure. 'Fore I even knew what happened, my right hand came up and pushed the pistol muzzle against his temple. Boz reached over and grabbed at my shirtsleeve just as I pulled the trigger and blasted most of Nate Coffin's brains all over the landing outside his imposing glass door. Made one hell of a mess. Corpse went over on its side like all the bones had been snatched out of the body at the same time.

Still shook all over as I stood. Holstered the still-smoking pistol and heard Ox say, "Damnation, Dodge. Thought I'd known some hard cases in my time. Acquainted with a few rumored to be about two shades meaner than the devil hisself. Good men not to mess with. But I'd swear 'fore a resurrected Jesus, ain't never seen one to match you, boy. Yep, be willin' to place my hand on the Good Book and testify as how I personally know that Lucius 'By God' Dodge is meaner'n hell with the hide off."

Boz just shook his head and said, "Mighta got a bit more out of 'im if'n you'd of put off killin' him just a mite longer, Lucius."

"You boys can just lay it to rest. Ain't nobody gonna make me feel bad about this killin', no matter what gets said. Any man bold enough, and lawless enough, to sanction the murder of children, then kidnap women and send them into service in a Mexican bordello, don't deserve to breathe the same air as God-fearin', law-abidin' folk."

Boz scratched his chin. "Figured on killin' him myself, Lucius. All I'm sayin' is, we might've got more in the way of helpful information if'n you'd of waited just a few more minutes."

I turned to Ox. "You know where the place he mentioned is? The Yellow Flower?"

He shifted the Sharps to his shoulder and held it by the butt like a foot soldier on parade. "I'd be willin' to bet damned every man inside a hundred miles of Nuevo

Laredo knows how to find that place blind-folded and in his sleep."

"Good. Let's get saddled up and be on our way." Headed for Grizz and snatched up his reins.

Stepped into the stirrup as Boz said, "Nuevo Laredo's one helluva rough place, Lucius. Sure you wanna do this right now? Might be better to wait until we can raise some help. Maybe bring in a few more Rangers."

Boz and Ox stood together. Turnbow had moved the heavy rifle again. It rested across both shoulders. He held the piece in place with one hand on the barrel and the other on the stock. I urged Grizz up close so there wouldn't be any doubt about what I said.

"There's no time left, fellers. We gotta get down to Nuevo Laredo as fast as these animals can carry us. With the Good Lord as my witness, Dianna Savage won't stay in that rat's nest a minute longer'n it'll take me to get there. I've sworn an oath in my own heart. She won't suffer any longer'n it's gonna take me to find her."

'Bout a second before we put the spur to our animals, I added, "God help the man who gets in the way of me making good on that promise, 'cause I ain't gonna have no mercy on 'im."

15

". . . COULD BE CARRYIN' FIVE PISTOLS AND PRIMED TO DO MURDER."

My agitation and profoundly felt guilt over Dianna's abduction prodded me into a rump burner of a hundred-mile forced ride between Coffin's ranch and the lush, green banks of the Rio Grande. Under a cloudless, slate-blue sky that covered a windswept world baked bone-dry by a searing sun, we spent most of two long, hot, grimy days on the trail before arriving just about twilight.

Covered in a thick coat of sweaty grit and near wrung out, we sat our thirsty mounts on a gentle, grass-covered slope that overlooked the sluggish river. While barely four feet deep, the water appeared clear, cool, and inviting. Eventually we allowed the horses to drink, but with great care.

Punishing trip across some of the most inhospitable desert country imaginable had done nothing to alleviate the feelings of anxious dread I harbored for Dianna's prospects. In fact, an ever-growing litany of dire thoughts, punctuated by horrible dreams, had plagued me since the day she vanished. As time dragged on, seemed to me I became more tense, uneasy, and, in the process, more dangerous.

Actually believed, when the chase began, that Nate Coffin's blood would satisfy my unfettered rage. I couldn't have been more wrong in my assessment. Seemed to me that not finding her at the outlaw leader's ranch had simply made matters worse.

Ox loafed in his saddle and said, "You can sit your animal right here and see for fifty miles in any direction. Put a few clouds in the air and the sunsets are damned near glorious."

"Beautiful spot," I said.

"Right peaceful," Boz added.

"Well, it's all those things now," Ox said. "But the Comanche used this crossing into Mexico for thousands of years of bloody raids and reprisals not so long ago. Poor Mexican peons damned sure suffered somethin' awful till us Texicans subdued them red devils. 'Course, I doubt they would ever admit such."

"We got much farther to ride?" I asked.

"Nuevo Laredo's across the river and down to the south a bit. We're still a few miles northwest. Rough *pueblecito* sits directly across the river from Laredo."

Boz threw a long, weary leg over his saddle horn, pulled makings, and set to rolling a smoke. Between puffs he said, "Whatever we do, boys, cain't let the bucolic appearance or God-granted beauty of this slow-moving place lull us into a false sense of safety. Every burro-leadin' son of a bitch down here's armed and hates gringo lawmen. Especially Texas Rangers. Worst cutthroats amongst 'em is likely workin' for this feller Bejarano."

His blunt assessment of our situation surprised me some. "You really think so, Boz? Figured sure this would be a lot easier confrontation than the one we just had with Nate Coffin."

"Tell you the truth, Lucius. We'd best take the time to get loaded for bear. Shotguns at the ready when we enter town — plenty of extra shells at hand. Every pistol with bullets in all chambers. None of that five-shooter, save-me-from-possibly-woundin'-myself-in-the-foot horseshit. We're gonna need fully packed and focused firepower at every turn."

Ox flicked a finger in the direction of my chest. "You boys might consider takin' them badges off too."

"Why would we want to do that?" I asked.

"Boz hit the nail right on its rusty head, Lucius. If they's one thing folks down this way hate, with an unbridled, blood-lettin' passion, it's the Texas Rangers. You boys show up on the streets of Nuevo Laredo sportin' them handmade shoot-me-right-now signs, and we'll all be dead as rotten stumps long 'fore we can even make it to the Yeller Flower."

Boz said, "Well, it's gettin' late. Don't know 'bout either of you, but I ain't real anxious about tryin' this raid in the dark. We're close enough now. Might as well rest the horses. Use some time to clean our weapons. Make sure they're primed and ready. Given the way we look and smell, might even be a good idea to bathe ourselves in the river."

Didn't need much in the way of encouragement when any opportunity to bathe came up. Dragged myself off Grizz, stripped down, and fell into the Rio Grande like a dead tree. Felt much better after.

Spent the rest of that evening, and late into that night, getting prepared for the next day's assault. Talked it over some more and decided we'd enter town from three different directions.

Lit by a flickering campfire, Ox drew a crude map in the sand, and went over various routes in an effort to make sure everyone understood how to arrive at our objective. "We'll be a lot less likely to draw unwanted attention this way. We go in three abreast, bristling with weapons, every peon south of the border'll know we're comin' within a few minutes. Have to use our watches. Work it just right. That way we can mosey through town separate and pretty much unobserved. Meet out front of Bejarano's joint together. Then we'll all waltz in at the same time. Really give 'em what fer."

Boz glanced up at his friend. "Got any ideas about what we'll find, Ox? Reckon we're in for much of a fight?"

"You know as much as I do. Never can tell about these places. One day, the joint could be as empty as an Arizona water gourd in July. Next day, a man might have to wait outside for his turn to get drunk and fornicate. Another day won't find an hombre who's armed. Then again, every man within a hundred miles could be carryin' five pistols and primed to do murder. Either way, this ain't gonna be easy."

"How so?" I asked.

"Well, Lucius, I don't think gettin' to the Flower will prove much of a problem. But once we've got Mrs. Savage in hand, gettin' out and makin' our way back across the river alive could well turn into a real challenge. Best prepare yourself for one blisterin' gunfight, boys. Soon as the shootin' starts, every vaquero in Nuevo Laredo is gonna be tryin' his level best to kill all of us deader'n Hell at a Baptist tent meetin'."

Our old amigo's ominous warnings had a profoundly off-putting effect on me that night. Couldn't sleep worth a wagonload of shucks. Even when I did manage to close tired eyes, blood-soaked dreams of terror and death filled my restless efforts at slumber. Rolled out of my lumpy bedding the next morning, and felt like someone had stood over my restless body and beat on me with a singletree from a Concord coach all night long.

Had an abbreviated meal of tough jerky and bad coffee before the sun got up good. Waded our animals across the shallow barrier between Texas and its poverty-stricken sister and pointed them south.

Came upon the edge of town pretty quick. Boz and Ox skirted on around to the west while I found a shady spot. Lit myself a smoke and waited an extra thirty minutes.

As soon as the time seemed right, pulled my shotgun from its bindings and checked the loads for the final time. Balanced it across my saddle as me and Grizz ambled our way into the rough village along a narrow, rock-hard, rutted trail that crossed a number of similar mazelike lanes. Closely hemmed in on either side by featureless, crumbling, dust-covered adobe houses set cheek by jowl, the cramped streets gave me a severe case of the creeping spooks.

Skinny, frightened dogs dressed in dull brown or mottled yellow fur appeared, showed their stained teeth, barked, and, just as quickly, vanished. Hardly any people out and about that fateful morning save the occasional big-eyed, runny-nosed child. Didn't matter. Still got the uncomfortable feeling of being constantly watched before I reached the main thoroughfare and headed west.

Turned the corner and spotted Ox as he made his way in from the opposite direction. Within seconds, Boz appeared from the south.

We followed Turnbow's lead. The three of us converged out front of one of the only free-standing, two-story buildings constructed from cut lumber. Painted in a bright, liquid green, trimmed in vivid pink, a blind man couldn't have missed it. Even that early in the morning, drunken laughter and ear-piercing trumpet music poured from behind a set of bloodred batwings and into the street.

Boldly lettered sign left no doubt we'd arrived at the right place. The most realistic painted yellow rose I'd ever seen decorated a background that matched the color on the doors. Stepped off our animals and, shoulder to shoulder, headed straight for the entrance. Boz took the center spot. I was on his left, Ox on the right.

Closer we got to the entryway, the louder the music and noisy celebration sounded. Stopped a step or two away from the interior of the combination cantina and whorehouse. Nodded nervous good-byes to each other, just in case that morning's job didn't work out in our favor. Pushed the swinging doors back and stepped inside. Ox and I quickly peeled off and we each headed for the closest corner.

Boz raised his big popper, cut loose, and blew a washtub-sized hole in the ceiling over the heads of the Yellow Flower's stunned and bug-eyed patrons. Concussion from the blast blew out the flame of a still-lit lamp that hung behind the bar. Thick puff of spent black powder rolled through the Mexican watering hole like a dark, churning wave on a storm-tossed lake. Entire place went so quiet you could hear your own hair grow.

Noise level, before we entered, belied the number of drunken revelers inside. I stood at the end of a fancy, out-of-place, well-shined bar that fully appeared to belong in a San Francisco saloon. Took a quick head count. Came up with seven men who all looked the part of hardened gunmen. They all sat at rude tables covered with bright, multicolored sarapes.

Bartender threw up his hands and backed as far away from me as he could get. The three-man band — a guitar plucker, fiddle player, and trumpet blower — was located against the far wall. They eased toward safety behind what was left of a battered upright piano.

Boz breeched his smoking weapon, re-loaded, snapped it closed, and pitched the spent brass away. Empty hit the floor with a hollow, metallic ring, and rolled toward an overflowing spittoon near the foot rail of the bar.

He threw a hot glance at the cowering drink wrangler and said, *"Habla ingles, amigo?"*

Terrified man's eyes darted from Boz to me and back again. "*Sí, señor.* A little." Word little came out sounding like leetle.

"Where's Alfonso Bejarano?"

"Que?"

Boz sounded quite a bit testier the second time around when he said, *"Donde está Alfonso Bejarano?"*

Man appeared so frightened he couldn't speak. Several times he attempted to make sounds that never came out. Finally he made the slightest of nervous motions. Lifted his shoulders as if to say, "I've got not a single idea on that particular subject."

Wound up tighter than the strings on a Missouri fiddle, I shook my shotgun at the same feller and demanded, *"Donde está la mujer americana?"* Must admit it surprised me' some when he raised a single, trembling finger and pointed to a spot somewhere above his head.

At the same time, the three of us shot a quick glance toward the stairs. Right quick I realized we'd have to go through every Mexican pistoleer in attendance to get where we had to go.

Took one step. Four of the hard-as-horseshoe-nails-looking carousers shoved ladder-backed chairs away from their tables and swayed to unsteady feet. Fiery, prickling sensation ran up my spine and, like an angry scorpion, found its way to my scalp. Knew in an instant they intended to fight. No backing down in those men.

As though previously agreed upon, they all went for their weapons. Do declare it was the damned stupidest thing I've ever seen that many people do at the same unthinking moment. Couldn't a one of them fellers been much smarter than half his hat size.

Have puzzled over the bloody events that followed for nearly a lifetime. Even after all these years, I could not truthfully testify in any court as to who fired the first shot. Think maybe Ox led the way, but might have been Boz, or maybe one of those chuckleheaded Mexican pistoleros. Didn't matter then and still don't. At any rate, Nuevo Laredo's ill-famed Yellow Flower erupted in a crescendo of general gunfire from both sides of the disagreement. Blasting sent everyone who had managed to live through the first barrage scurrying for cover behind anything at hand.

An invisible blade from six barrels of .10-gauge buckshot sliced through at least three of those Mexican gunmen like a sharpened scythe takes down sun-seared wheat. Tables, chairs, bottles, and men exploded. Flew into a spray of gore-saturated bits right before my eyes.

Quick as possible, I dropped to the floor. Lucked into a much-appreciated degree of safety behind the far end of the bar. Found I could load up, hold the shotgun around my sheltered spot, fire blindly at our adversaries, and repeat the process with little fear of being damaged. No real need to aim. Big, ole .10-gauge mowed down everything in front of its destruction-belching muzzle.

For what seemed like an eternity the continuous, unnerving, soul-shattering thunder from our big poppers, along with all the return fire from the pistols of our outgunned opponents, proved damned near deafening. Noise level led me to feel as though the vengeful hand of the true God had descended on that gaudy border-town booze locker and smacked it so hard the ceiling joists creaked, bent, and almost broke. My ears rang like cathedral bells. Dust from the ceiling, along with burnt black powder and loosened plaster, rained down on everyone.

Guess we'd got about a minute and a half into red-eyed, murderous blasting when the deadly dance started to let up a bit. Of a sudden, I heard Boz yell at me over an unimpressive series of staccato pistol shots fired our direction. Was damn near deaf from all the gunfire that'd been squeezed into the room. Against my overly abused eardrums, he sounded like a man at the bottom of an Arkansas well.

Took a second or so before I spotted him through the thick screen of vaporized blood and hanging filth, filled with death.

"You still livin', Lucius?" he yelled.

"Not so much as a scratch so far," I yelled back. "How 'bout Ox?"

Could barely see Boz flash a toothy grin through the haze. Boz yelped, "You couldn't kill that man with a sledgehammer and forty whacks."

Random shots from a single remaining opponent eventually petered out. Several minutes of near complete quiet, moans, Spanish entreaties I couldn't understand, and weeping, led us to gamble some, stand, and survey all the carnage we'd wrought.

God Almighty, but you'd of been sorely pressed to find a single stick of formerly existing furniture still intact. Glanced down and counted the empties at my feet. Appeared I'd ripped off near twenty loads of buckshot. Given that Boz and Ox most likely put an equal amount of hot lead in the air, astonished me that anything in front of our guns had managed to escape total annihilation.

Bartender peeked out at me, motioned upstairs again, and whispered, *La mujer americana es arriba, señor.*

Turned to Boz and said, "You boys take care of this mess. I'll find Dianna, and we'll get the hell out of here. Watch my back. Don't let anyone follow me up." They nodded, and I headed for the second floor.

Took those stairs two at a time. Landing opened into a dingy, unpainted hallway that ran from the back of the building to the front. Grit and filth from years of use decorated the walls.

Three doors located on either side of the passage faced each other like silent, hooded sentinels waiting for me to pass. A single portal remained closed — the last one on the left, before you reached a window that overlooked the street below.

As I made my way to the last entry on the left, several frightened, almost naked girls appeared. No older than thirteen or fourteen years of age, they squealed, darted from various hiding places, sprinted past me, and headed down the stairs.

Gingerly stepped up to the edge of my objective and squatted. Heartbeat and a half later, four shots fired from inside the room crashed through the flimsy wall and rough-plank door above my head.

Few seconds of quiet passed and a feller inside said, "You still alive, amigo?"

Stood, said, "Yeah," and ducked again.

More shots punched death-dealing holes above me. Hopped up, squared off, and kicked hell out of the board panel an inch or so right of the latch, and stepped inside. Dreadful sight I beheld damned near made me sick. Thought for a second I might puke my spurs up.

Lanky feller, all dressed in black, stood beside a filthy, broken-down bed and was locked in a single-minded attempt to reload his weapon. Those efforts stopped as soon as I flicked the muzzle of the shotgun his direction. He dropped the pistol, raised his hands, and stepped backward until the wall behind stopped his progress.

Tied to the sagging cot's iron frame lay the body of a stark naked and unconscious woman I barely recognized. Covered in filth, smeared blood, and God only knows what else, she appeared to have been beaten from the soles of her feet to her hairline. A swollen, bruised face sported blackened, closed eyes, a still-bleeding nose, and cut lips.

The sight of Dianna in such a state caused a rage in me unlike any I'd ever experienced.

16

". . . THERE'S GONNA BE HELL TO PAY."

Stood by that filthy bed, and for nigh on five seconds, I do believe my brain numbed up and went into some kind of seizure. Couldn't move. Couldn't think. Nothing left inside me but red-eyed fury. Wanted to storm Hell and bite Satan's horns off. Then, honest to God, it felt as though something inside my skull snapped like a rotten tree limb.

Snatched a grimy coverlet from a broke-backed chair and threw it over her nude, motionless body. Bent over and whispered in a blood-encrusted ear, "It's Lucius, Dianna. I've come for you. You gotta hold on now, darlin'. Get you out of here quick as I can."

Took every fiber of my being not to burst into torrents of hot, salty tears. Steadied my nerves, stood, and faced the man in black. Right sure he didn't have any doubt his life was on the line.

Lifted the shotgun so the muzzle pointed at his crotch. "Your name Bejarano?" I asked.

"No, sir. Oh, hell, no. That gutless son of a bitch skipped out yesterday. Left me and them boys downstairs to deal with any problems."

"Problems? You mean like me and my friends?"

"Swear 'fore Jesus, mister, we didn't have no idea gunfightin' fellers of yore caliber might show up. Alfonso said we could drink all we wanted, eat all we wanted, have some fun, or make use of the woman if'n we wanted."

"Make use of her? What the hell does that mean?"

"Well, think everyone here humped her a time or two, but she ain't been worth much since Alfonso beat the blue-eyed hell out of her. Just kinda lays there. Ain't a bit of fun. Kinda like screwin' a dead stump."

Almost sent him to Satan right when those reckless words fell from his filthy mouth. Couldn't believe any man living could be that stupid. He'd just heard me speak to Dianna. Watched and listened as I tried to comfort her.

Right testylike I snapped, "You know why I'm here?"

"Ain't got a single idea, mister. Don't care, not even one whit. Hell, I'm just a workin' man tryin' to make a dollar. Your life's labor don't interest me in the least. Sure you understand, don't you?"

Fished the badge out of my vest pocket and pinned it back on my chest. Gunny's eyes got big as saucers. "Now wait a minute, Ranger," he whimpered. "Didn't have no idea you wuz a full-blown Texas lawdog when I started shootin'. Just doin' as I'd been told by the *jefe*."

"I came for the woman. She's the only reason you're still alive and I'm talkin' to you right now."

Trembling lips stretched and revealed rotten teeth. Could hear the cracks in his voice when he whined, "Gotta believe me. Swear on my mother's grave, I got nothin' to do with the way she looks. Bastard Alfonso done all that. Said he'd been paid a handsome price to ruin her by some feller name of Coffin. Said this Coffin wanted him to make it so no man would ever look at her again."

My voice must have sounded about as sharp as a well-stropped razor when I said, "You or any of your friends downstairs try to stop 'im? Do anything to keep what I see here from happenin'?"

He blinked like I'd slapped him. "W-w-we had no say a'tall in the matter. Swear to God, Ranger, w-w-we 'uz just carryin' out orders."

"That include everyone here takin' a turn at rapin' this poor, defenseless girl?"

Dumb bastard tried to make it sound like we were old friends. Got all personal-like. "Well, now, that didn't amount to any more'n an added benefit, as you might say. Just somethin' extra to enhance some pretty poor pay."

Couldn't believe the nervy son of a bitch. Spoke to me like I should understand, and then grinned real big right in my face.

That's when I dropped the shotgun's hammer. Peppered him all the way from knee to crotch. Thunderous blast picked the worthless piece of scum up, threw his flopping body against the wall. Splattered most of his privates all over Hell and yonder. He slid to the floor in a bloody, twitching heap. Didn't kill him, but sure as hell came close. Knocked the son of a bitch stone-cold unconscious for a bit.

As I worked at wrapping a limp, battered Dianna in the ratty coverlet, he came back around, grabbed at the spot where his missing equipment once resided, and screamed like a panther with a red-hot poker up its butt. Never had heard such a pitiable sound come out of a living man's mouth. Kind of shrieking screech had the power to pull tears out of a sideshow freak's glass eye.

Within a matter of seconds, footfalls thundered up the stairway. Boz burst in ready for a fight, and glanced around the room. Motioned for him to give me some help. We worked together, and eventually got Dianna into a sitting position on the edge of the bed. From there, I lifted the shattered girl into my good friend's arms.

Grabbed his elbow and fixed him in my best hardcase lawdog gaze. "Get her out of this hellhole, Boz. Want you and Ox to head for the river as fast as you can hoof it. Don't look back. Cross over quick as you can. Take her straight to the nearest doctor. I'll finish up here, follow, and cover your rear. Find you when I'm done."

"Damn, Lucius, we ain't gonna leave you in this place alone. Soon's word gets around that a bunch of murderin' gringos just come to town and kilt some local boys, there's gonna be hell to pay. Should be happenin' pretty quick."

"We don't have time to debate this, Boz. You gotta do as I say. Take Dianna and get to Laredo. She needs professional medical attention in the worst kinda way. Get movin'. Do it now."

He frowned, and then shook his head. Said, "All right. I'm goin'. Don't like it much, my friend, but I'm goin'."

Kissed Dianna on the forehead. Doubt she heard me when I whispered, "Boz'll take care of you, darlin'. I'll be comin' along shortly." Slapped my amigo on the shoulder and pushed him toward the door.

"You watch yourself, Lucius. Anything happens to you, I'll come back and kill you myself." He grinned; then they disappeared down the smoke-filled hallway.

With a load of guilt on my shoulders the size of a Mississippi riverboat, I kneeled beside the wounded gunman and rolled a cigarette. Screeching pain had turned into something akin to mute shock. He stared blank-eyed at the ceiling, moaned pitifully, and trembled all over.

Knew beyond any doubt the poor bastard was well on the way to bleeding out right where he fell. From the pasty-white appearance of his face, I figured he had but a few agonizing minutes left amongst the living — at the outside.

Leaned over and stuck the burning cigarette between his twitching lips. He took part of a puff. Went on a hacking, coughing rip, and spit the smoking butt onto his wet, sticky, wine-colored lap.

"Well, cowboy, you've branded your last calf, had your final glass of liquor, danced your last jig, and abused your very last woman. 'Fore you wake up shoveling coal in Satan's soul-sizzlin' furnaces, I want you to tell me where Bejarano lives. Maybe do a little toward redeemin' yourself for past sins."

Wild tormented eyes flicked up at me. Barely heard him gasp, "You can go straight to a burnin' Hell yourself."

Pulled a pistol and cocked it. "Tell me what I want to know and I'll help you on over to the other side. Put you out of your misery. Carry on with this stupid act, and you're gonna keep sufferin' somethin' awful. Slap bleed to death right where you sit. That could take several more hours of merciless agony."

Hell, I knew it was a bald-faced lie. He was already dead. Just hadn't figured it out yet. Personally, I couldn't have cared less about his situation. Belly-slinkin' snake had information I wanted.

Rheumy, bloodshot eyes rubbered around in a lolling head that appeared as though attached to his body with a piece of limp rawhide. Had to slap him back awake at least twice. Never cared for beating on a man so near death, but I began to fear he wouldn't stay alive long enough to provide me with some much-needed information.

Finally had to smack him real good and hard. All at once, he got clearheaded. In a bloody gasp, he shot back, "Go ahead and end it, you badge-wearin' bastard. Likes of you been tryin' to kill me ever since I turned twelve years old. Year I kilt Ma and Pa. Might as well git this dance over with and done." Then he made a frothy, liquid-saturated, strangling noise, groaned, and passed out again.

Grabbed a pitcher of questionable-looking water from the only table in the room, snatched his hat off, and poured the entire jug over his sweat-saturated head. Shock snapped him away from death's doorstep one final time.

Grabbed his bloody shirtfront and shook him. "Gonna keep bringin' you back to life till you tell me where Bejarano lives."

"Not sure." Sounded like a man on his way to the bottom of a well when he stuttered out, "Stays on American side. Safer for . . . his . . . family. Biggest . . . house . . . in Laredo. See it from . . . this side. Bright . . . red roof. Can't miss . . ."

He made a kind of huffing sound. Spit up a handful of blood. Startled eyes rolled up into the back of his head. Then he flopped into a gory, tub-sized pool that spread across the nasty floor toward the toes of my boots.

Holstered my pistol and grabbed the shotgun. Checked the loads and headed for the stairs at a trot. Got to the landing on the first floor and surveyed the destruction we'd wrought.

God above, but we'd made one hell of a mess that day. Couple of them Mexican boys as we shot in our initial assault died right where they fell. Them who managed to live were being attended by a swarming group of excited, chattering women who'd fogged into the cantina after Boz took off.

One of those angry *mujers* spotted me. As if on signal, they all went to pointing my direction and hollering in Spanish. Couldn't understand much of what got said, but it sounded a lot like swear words.

Backed my way out the batwing doors. Shouts, jeering, curses, and flying debris followed. My friends had left Grizz tied near the Yellow Flower's entrance. Animal snorted when I jumped aboard. Appeared to me as though he wanted away from all the noise and destruction of that border cantina as quick as I could make it happen.

Kicked for the first street that headed

toward the river. Hadn't quite turned the corner when the shooting started again. Just a few potshots here and there at first. Glanced over my shoulder and spied half a dozen uniformed *federales* hoofin' it my direction. Mexican *soldados* fired as they ran. Bullets peppered the dirt, chinked the adobe walls of the buildings closest to me, and gouged holes in wooden porches and trim. One slug put a crease along Grizz's rump and set him to rearing.

Jumped off and led the skittish animal to cover around a corner, then returned fire. Not my intention to kill any Mexican lawmen if I could help it. But I knew they wouldn't quit coming unless I gave them something serious to think on.

As best I could, retreated toward the Rio Grande and safety. Kept Grizz close and maintained a constant barrage of return fire. Whole dance got pretty hairy along the way. Angry Mexican folks even went to chuckin' garbage at me from above when I took shelter under their balconies.

Intense, door-to-door, running gun battle lasted almost a quarter of a mile. Finally, had to gamble some. Jumped back on Grizz, kicked hard for the water, and the hoped-for safety on the other side. A hailstorm of blue whistlers cut through the air. Hot lead fell all around, so thick I'm still amazed me and the horse made the riverbank alive.

Dropped off into some thick bushes hard by the river's edge. Decided if I wanted to stay alive, was gonna have to get serious about driving my pursuers away. Pulled my rifle, shotgun, and three full cartridge belts of ammunition. Set Grizz loose and watched him pick his way down the tree- and scrub-covered slope to the water's slow-moving edge. Knew he wouldn't wander far.

Found a nice spot of cover at the base of some cottonwoods. Waited until some of those Mexican fellers came into the open area between Nuevo Laredo's first group of adobes and my hidey-hole. Got a clear shot. Put two of them down right quick. Had the exact effect I wanted. Whole whooping, hollering bunch dragged their wounded friends away and retreated back into the safety of the village.

For about three hours — till just before dark anyway — we traded shots here and there. Time or two, a feller on their side of the dispute would get nervy and start hot-footing it my direction. But none ever got very close. I'd put a nick or two in them as ventured into the open. Then some of their friends would come out and drag them back.

Third or fourth time it happened, struck me as kind of funny. Guess they heard me laughing. Must have made them boys madder than a nest of those monstrous, orange-colored Mexican hornets. They poured a curtain of hot lead in on me, but never did hit anything.

'Bout the time night came down like thunder, spotted someone swimming a horse from the American side of the river. Got close enough, and I could tell it was Boz. He and his pony came up on the muddy bank right beside Grizz.

Heard him whisper, "Dodge. You still alive, boy?"

Stepped out of the bushes. Said, "Damned good to see you, old friend. Glad you came back for me."

He stepped down, rushed over, and grabbed me like a long-lost brother. Hugged my neck and, in a voice filled with emotion, said, "Had to wait till it got some dark, you know. Would've been too dangerous otherwise. Damn, Lucius, thought you wuz a goner, son. From what I could see through my long glass, figured these Mexican fellers had done went and kilt the hell out of you."

Pushed him back. "Don't have a scratch on me. Let's get mounted, my friend. We gotta get the hell outta here right now.

Would bet the ranch these *federales* are gonna overrun this place in another few minutes. They've been waitin' all day long for dark to come too."

We got mounted and urged our animals into the cool, dark water. Boz headed out first. I followed. Held on and swam the horses toward the safety of the *Estados Unidos.*

Our retreat went right well till about halfway across. Then bullets went to falling around us like raindrops. But darkness, distance, and fatigue must have taken their toll on the shooters. Thank God them fellers weren't able to do us any damage.

Soon as we pulled up on the Laredo side of the river, I stepped down and watched as men on the other side kept firing at anything moving. "Don't appear they're willing to give up on this shindig, does it?"

Boz slapped me on the back. "Mexicans are a determined folk when they get stirred up the right way, Lucius. Hope you've learned something from this little raid."

"Oh, I learned plenty. Now, where's Dianna?"

Even in the dark I could tell he hated to answer the question. "Well, I got her put up with a doc like you said. Stayed with the girl right up till I came lookin' for you, son."

"You left her alone in a strange place?"

"No. No. Nothin' like that. Needn't worry yourself, my friend. Ox stayed with her. Told him he'd best not let anything more happen to the girl."

Exhaustion fell on me like a railroad locomotive dropped from heaven. "Sweet Jesus, Boz, it's been an awful day. So tired I'm gettin' stupid. Forgot about Ox. Did the doc say anything about how she's doin'?" Deep down I knew exactly what he would say. But knowing is one thing; hearing bad news for certain is something else altogether.

"Not really. But I gotta tell ya, her situation don't look good. She's in mighty bad shape, Lucius."

17

"I INTEND TO KILL YOU EXTREMELY DEAD."

Dr. F. Scott Bryles had a practice in Laredo about three blocks from the river. Small, stuffy, and filled with medical books in stacked, glass-fronted cases, the room where he'd laid Dianna out felt like the inside of a living animal.

Half-burned candle flickered on a table beside her bed. Dancing light threw a ghastly glow across a pale, badly bruised face. Antiseptic smells of alcohol, carbolic, and other things I didn't recognize swept over me in a wave that singed the hairs in my nose. Pungent odors slipped into my lungs, squeezed all the fresh air out, and brought hot tears to my tired eyes.

Stepped inside, hat in hand, and almost passed out right on the spot. I'd thought for sure once a good pill roller got her cleaned up, treated all her obvious wounds and such, she'd come back from the other side and be herself again. When real love hits,

Jesus, but a man can certainly fool himself with false hope.

Nothing I'd seen, or done, since her disappearance prepared me for the way she looked. Not even finding her tied naked to a bed in Nuevo Laredo. Wrapped in a white sheet from chin to foot, the beautiful girl, who'd inspired unquenchable feelings of love and lust in me with so little effort, appeared dead and ready for burial.

Slumped into a chair crammed up beside the medical couch where she lay, and damn near wept. Remember thinking at the time that her entire head appeared swollen and bereft of anything like the color you'd expect in a living face. The once-flawless skin I'd kissed with such fervor and affection gave off a distinctly yellowish-blue tint — except those spots where the bruises and abrasions looked the worst. Detected knuckle marks on the cheek I could see best in the poor light. Couldn't imagine the suffering she'd endured and managed, somehow, to survive.

Honest to God, it appeared as though she would surely drown in her own sweat. A glistening sheen drenched her face and hair and soaked the pillow beneath her head. Took less than a minute for me to make up my mind exactly what I had to do.

Hopped up and headed for the door. Barely crossed the threshold and almost ran into Boz and Ox. Said, "I'm gonna rent a coach and take her to Fort Worth."

Boz looked like I'd slapped him. "Damn, Lucius. That's more'n four hundred miles."

"We'll take our time. Go at it easy."

Ox took me by the elbow. "Gotta think of the girl, Lucius." Sounded like my father trying to convince me not to jump off the roof of the barn.

"Am thinking of her. Dianna Savage saved my life. Wasn't for her, I'd of long since been worm food. If this poor girl hadn't stepped up to the situation when no one else did, she probably wouldn't be lyin' in there like a corpse. I'll hire someone to take care of her. Hell, I'll hire Dr. Bryles if he's willing to make the trip."

"Why don't we talk with the doc first, Lucius?" Boz tried to sound reasonable, but he knew me well enough to understand that I'd already made up my mind and nothing anyone else could say would change it.

"Sure as shootin'. Get 'im in here. Don't mind talkin', but when the talkin's done, we're headin' to Fort Worth — whether he goes along for the trip or not."

Fine feller, Doc Bryles. Short, dark, and intense. He said, "Lady's physical injuries are abundant. Those might take weeks, perhaps months, to heal. But I have to be truthful and say also that some of her wounds may never mend. Whoever gave her the beating knew exactly where to hit a person to do the most painful damage. And while all that's bad enough, it's her mental condition that concerns me most."

His assessment struck me as a reasonable, studied, and educated way to look at Dianna's condition. Think we must've all said, "Mental condition?" at the same time.

He tapped pince-nez glasses against his thumb. "I could be wrong in my appraisal, of course, but it appears her mind might be more profoundly injured than her body."

Ox surprised me when he said, "Could the beatin' have damaged her brain, Doc? I've seen folks what got hit in the head who were never the same again. Feller worked on my ranch few years back got kicked over the eye by a horse. Turned a right nice young man into a slobberin' idiot."

Bryles shook his head. "Not certain how severe Mrs. Savage's injures are. No way to know for sure just how badly she's hurt. Only time will tell."

"Can't you even venture a guess?" I asked.

He glanced at me for about a second, then looked down at his feet. "If she's not better in two or three weeks, I doubt seriously her situation will ever improve very much. Have to wait until she regains consciousness before we can really tell much. But you should be aware, gentlemen, my examination thus far doesn't hold out much hope."

A week later we'd obtained a wagon, hired a traveling companion for Dianna, and bought plenty of provisions for the trip. At the same time, I'd done some snooping and found Alfonso Bejarano's home. Surprised the hell out of me when I discovered it was located but a pleasant five-minute walk from Doc Bryles's office.

Spent every free second away from Dianna's bedside watching the place. Eight-foot-high adobe walls made seeing inside right difficult. But through subtle questioning of neighbors, and local vendors who often visited the residence, I soon had a fairly detailed diagram of the main house and an assured, easy method of gaining entry.

A number of Laredo's affable hawkers pointed out for me the very person of the benevolent and generous Señor Bejarano. The infamous borderland bandit, killer, and pimp made almost daily rounds to various street stands while buying vegetables, visiting, and such. Man acted as though the world remained his own personal oyster.

Found myself stunned by the despicable weasel's appearance. I had expected a full-fledged, heavily moustachioed, bandolier-draped *bandido* of the first water. What befell my heated gaze was a dark-eyed, short, thin, well-dressed *jefe* given to a regal and pompous demeanor. His observable conduct bespoke a man who obviously thought himself safe from any harm on the American side of the Rio Grande.

Surprised and pleased me that I could detect no bodyguard in evidence at his dwelling, nor did any accompany him during his afternoon shopping jaunts. When I cautiously inquired as to the advisability of Bejarano walking the streets unaccompanied, an affable taco dealer informed me, "Our *patrón* has nothing to worry himself about here in Laredo, Señor. *La gente* know what would happen if they should bring him, or any member of his family, to harm. He is perfectly safe."

Rumors swirled amongst the peons that virtually every man under Bejarano's employ searched northern Mexico for a band of killers who'd raided one of his extensive properties in Nuevo Laredo. Most people observed that, although the gringo marauders had managed to escape, Señor Bejarano appeared convinced that additional murderous brigands still lurked somewhere south of the Rio Grande and meant to do the great man extreme harm.

Much to my surprise, and satisfaction, I also discovered that Señora Bejarano and her two sons had traveled to Mexico City some weeks before our arrival to visit with the lady's ailing mother. But for a few servants, Alfonso Bejarano's house appeared empty. That pleasant news made what I had in mind considerable easier.

Night before we left town and headed north for Fort Worth, got the wagon packed and set up as best we could for Dianna's comfort. Bided my time. Waited until my friends had drifted off to sleep, and then I slipped away.

Less than half an hour later, I carefully pushed a chair against the door to Bejarano's night chamber and took a seat beside his bed. Huge, deathly pale moon lit the room like daylight. Could have easily reached out and touched the sleeping man.

Pulled a pistol and laid it in my lap atop a fringed pillow I'd found in the chair. Fished out the makings and rolled a cigarette. When I scratched a lucifer to life and sucked in a deep and satisfying lungful of the tobacco smoke, the object of my attention sat up in a wild-eyed panic.

He snatched the sheets to a trembling chin. Surprised me some when a high, thin voice squeaked, *"Quien es?"*

I'd never been as calm in my entire life. In as quiet and soothing a voice as I could muster up, said, *"Habla inglés, Señor Bejarano?"* Took a puff and blew the smoke in his face.

Man swallowed hard and blurted out, "Yes. I speak passable English. My many businesses on this side of the border require it."

"Heard on the streets as how your family is in Mexico visiting relatives. That right?"

"Sí. Yes. Yes. *Es muy correcto,"* he stammered.

"You have any idea who I am? Why I'm here?"

"No. No, *señor.* I do not. A thief, I suppose."

"Oh, no. I'm not a thief. Came here to rescue a friend of mine. Lady named Savage. She was brought to you against her will. Imprisoned at the Yellow Flower in Nuevo Laredo by men in the employ of you and Nate Coffin."

He shook his head and looked right sneaky. "I know nothing of this, *señor. Nada. Cero.* Nothing at all."

"Then you know nothing of Coffin's untimely recent departure from this life to a preferred spot in Satan's fiery pit?"

"While my English *is* passable, *señor,* I do not understand what you've just said."

"Well, let me see if I can enlighten you. Your friend Nate Coffin is no longer living, sir. I killed the son of a bitch. Shot him dead after he told me who held Mrs. Savage and where to find her."

In the soft glow that flooded the room and lapped against all its furnishings, Bejarano's chestnut-colored face went pale and pasty. Black eyes darted to the Colt lying in my lap, up to my face, and thence to the bedroom door.

"Not a chance in hell," I said. "So don't try it. Gonna have to just sit here and take the consequences of your actions like a man."

"Is it your intent to kill me, *señor?*"

"Oh, without a doubt, you evil old bastard. I intend to kill you extremely dead."

Terrified skunk flinched as though I'd slapped him. "You cannot mean that. Alfonso Bejarano is an individual of great importance in Laredo. I am acquainted with many of your type. Even one with your brutal background would never murder an unarmed gentleman, in his bed, at a time

281

when he has completed his nightly prayers and is closest to God."

"Normally you'd be right, Señor. But not in this particular instance. You see, Mrs. Savage enjoys a very special place in my heart. What you and your men did to her, you son of a bitch, can only be described as unforgivable. Such brutality cannot be dismissed. And will be avenged right here, tonight, before I leave."

He got a bit nervy and sneered, "I have no fear of death. You can do as you will. But be aware, sir, my men will search to the ends of time to find you. They will kill you, as well as your entire family."

"Seriously doubt your hired killers'll care all that much once you're gone. And besides, no one's gonna ever know exactly what happened here tonight, or who did the world a favor by erasin' your shadow from the earth."

He lowered the sheet and talked to me as though lecturing a small child. "A proposition perhaps? I am the wealthiest man in Laredo and all of northern Mexico. I can pay you enough to live on for the rest of your life, if you are willing to reconsider."

"I have no need of money. From the look of things right now, you've already taken from me what I needed more than anything else in the world. Not sure I can ever get it back."

He shook his head as though he still did not comprehend. "Men such as ourselves always appreciate the ways of the world. This *incident* amounted to nothing more than a business arrangement. Señor Coffin needed, I think you would call it, a consideration. Yes, a consideration for which he was willing to pay a handsome price."

"A handsome price?"

"Yes. So you see, so far as I was concerned, the woman amounted to little more than a job. A job easily performed."

"Like all those other young girls who work in the Yellow Flower?"

"Exactly. Had everything gone as planned, by this time next week, Mrs. Savage would have been nothing more than a Nuevo Laredo whore available to anyone for the purchase price of a handful of pesos."

"A handful of pesos?"

"A man must make a living. I have an extensive family. Many relatives. Their needs are great. But for the interference of you and your friends, I expected to make money off Mrs. Savage, coming and going."

"Physical assault, savage rape, and turning women and young girls to the damnation of whoredom are hardly what any Christian person would call business as usual, or nothing more'n a job, you blaspheming son of a bitch."

Figured we'd talked long enough. Covered my pistol with the throw pillow. Muffled first shot hit him dead center — about three inches above the notch in his breastbone. Like a doubled-up fist, the .45 slug knocked him backward into his bedding.

Shocked and surprised, he tried to suck air into uncooperative lungs — but to no avail. Evil skunk wheezed, coughed, and spit up an egg-sized wad of gore. Ripped his nightshirt back and fumbled at the black-rimmed, oozing hole with clumsy fingers that had turned into shovels.

Calm as a horse trough in a drought, I leaned a bit closer and said, "As my father liked to say, Señor, 'You just went and committed an error in judgment that by God takes the cake.' "

As the horror of imminent death gained purchase in his already dying brain, he glared up at me, gritted his teeth, and took the second shot right between the eyes. Splatter of bone, blood, and hair made a hell of a mess on the bed's hand-carved wooden headboard. Shot knocked his noggin backward into a pillow quickly ruined by the jumble of brain matter that leaked out the hole in back of his head.

Stood and gazed down at the corpse just long enough to make sure he was deader than Santa Anna. Taste of copper floated over the bed on a cloud of spent gunpowder. Air groaned its way out of Bejarano's limp body for some seconds. When the sounds of approaching death finally stopped, I holstered my pistol. Figured there was no point wasting another .45 slug on his sorry ass.

Knew then, as surely as I know now, some softhearted, softheaded folks would condemn me for the way I'd dealt with Coffin and Bejarano. Those people have most likely never seen someone they loved, and held dear to their hearts, rashly murdered or appallingly violated. And until they do, the mushy-minded and feeble-brained can take their opinions and go straight to a burning, festerated Hell as far as I'm concerned.

Pitched the pillow aside, slipped out of an open window in Bejarano's bedchamber, and disappeared into the night. A troop of yelling servants thundered up the stairs right behind me. I hit the street unmolested, and strolled back to Doc Bryles's place like a man on his way to Sunday school. For the first time since the moment I'd found

Dianna in Nuevo Laredo, felt like the world had almost righted itself in the heavens again.

Epilogue

Amid the general hubbub generated by the murder of one of Laredo's leading citizens, Boz and I said our good-byes to Ox Turnbow the next morning. Man allowed as how he missed his ranch and couldn't wait to get back. Can't say that I blamed him none. Old Ranger had fought well and fearlessly. Shook his hand, climbed into the wagon, and headed out. Boz lingered a bit longer. Turned and saw those brave souls hug and slap each other's shoulders like brothers. 'Bout as much as you can expect from men as hard as those two.

Honest to God, felt like the trip back to Fort Worth lasted forever. Dianna improved not one bit and, according to her companion and my own observations, even appeared to get worse. 'Course we stopped several places along the way for two and three days at a stretch. Even visited with my mother in Waco for almost a week. Good woman tried to help, but nothing any of us did seemed to have the least effect on the injured girl's mental well-being.

Once we made Fort Worth, I put her up in Blackstock's Convalescent Home down on Throckmorton Street, not far from St. Stanislaus Catholic Church. Fancified doctor name of Buckholzer, who claimed to have been educated back East, tried his hand with her. He didn't make any real progress either.

In the beginning, I did my level best to visit with the broken girl several times during any week that did not find me out beating the bushes for thieves and killers. And while Dianna's physical injuries and overall appearance improved with the passage of time, nothing of this world appeared to touch her vacant, dead-eyed look.

Eventually, I sent for Dr. Hardin Q. Puckett, from over at Willow Junction. Given his Civil War experiences, and success with MaryLou Wainwright, thought sure he could help mend Dianna's stricken mind. He stayed over and worked with her for more than a month. Refused to accept any payment for his trouble. Mighty nice of the man. Sadly, his valiant efforts all came to naught.

As my daddy liked to say, you can't hold

back time. Days turned into weeks, weeks into months, months into years. Through considerable legal wrangling, and eventually by the personal intervention of Cap'n Wag Culpepper, I got myself declared executor of Dianna's extensive estate so I could see to her proper care. Only once during all that time, worry, and turmoil did I see the spark of life return to that beautiful, broken girl.

Stopped in for a visit late one afternoon following a particularly difficult chase that took me all the way to Kansas and back. Gold-tinted light from the setting sun flooded the room and touched her stunning face like a lover's kiss sent straight from God. Flopped into a chair beside her bed and, after some few minutes, must have dozed off. Awoke with a start and noticed that she was staring at me. First real response I'd seen.

Stunned hell out of me when she smiled, reached out, and caressed my hand. "Soon," she said. "Not now, but soon, dear Lucius."

Girl hadn't spoken a word in all the years since the horror of Nuevo Laredo. You cannot imagine my happiness at the time. Unfortunately, she leaned back into her pillow and, as far as I am aware, never said another word for the rest of her life.

Almost exactly a year to the very day she

last spoke to me, Dianna closed her eyes for the final time and died. Her nurses and doctors could do little but shake their heads. Typical of medical practice back then, they were properly baffled. Perplexed. Mystified. Had no idea what brought her to such a sad end.

Buried the beautiful Dianna in Fort Worth's Oakwood Cemetery. Put a very distinctive marble angel at the head of the grave. Weeping creature kneels over her resting place to this very day. You can still see it — if you take the time to look. Had young William moved up from Salt Valley and placed in a spot beside her. Figured she would want him with her for their eternal rest.

Now, so many years later, here I sit beside a stoked-up tin stove, tears streaming down my leathery cheeks, trying to stay warm. Just a broken-down old Ranger, whiskey glass in hand, alone, with nothing left but my dreams and memories.

I've heard other antique people go on and on about how wonderful memories are. Can't swear to that myself. Because, to tell the truth, friends, I'd trade *all* my memories for a mere fifteen minutes of lying in bed beside Dianna and the heavenly opportunity to taste her breath in my mouth again when she kissed me.

Would gladly give up my own life with both hands this very second for such a blissful prospect.